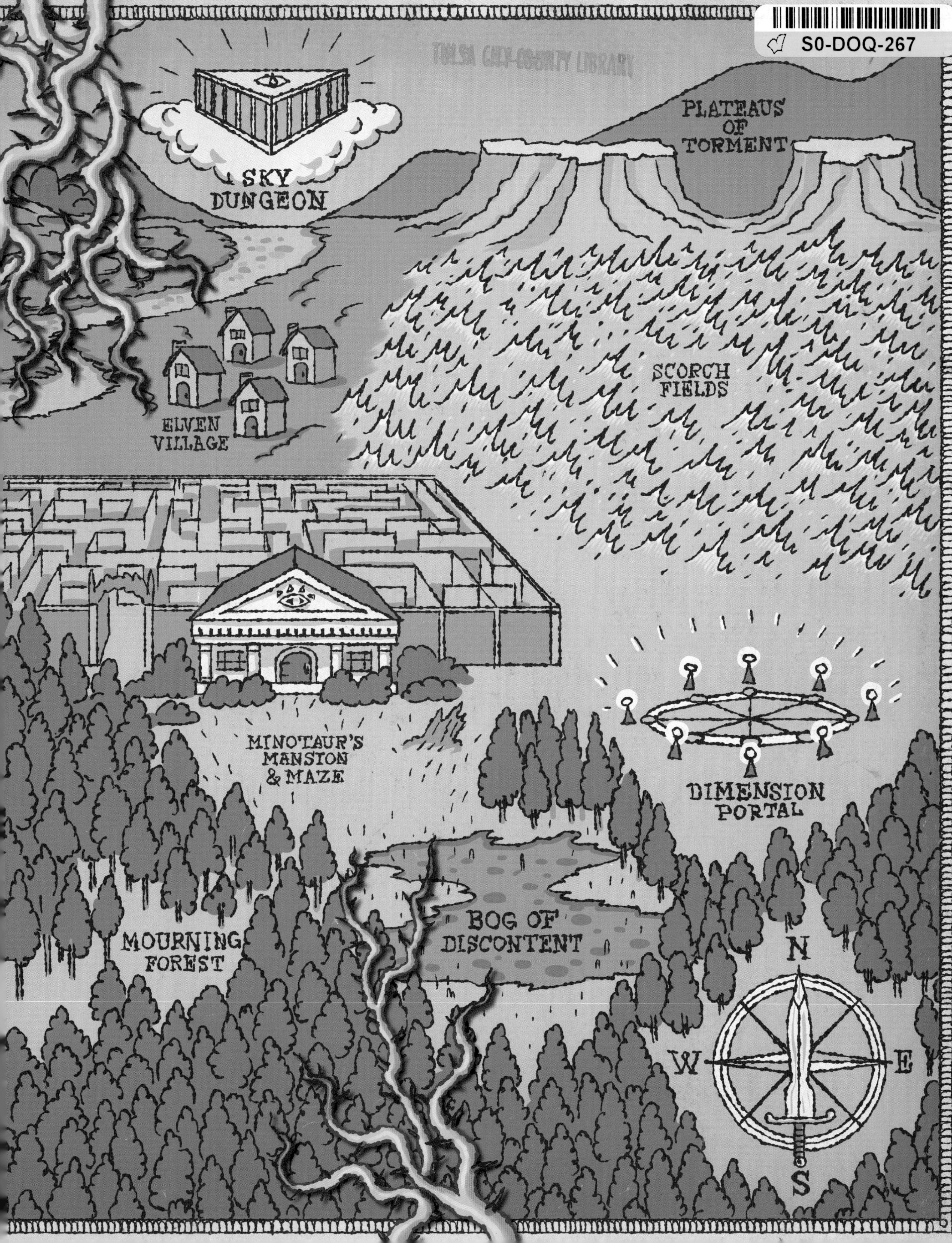
SKY DUNGEON
PLATEAUS OF TORMENT
SCORCH FIELDS
ELVEN VILLAGE
MINOTAUR'S MANSION & MAZE
DIMENSION PORTAL
MOURNING FOREST
BOG OF DISCONTENT
N
W
E
S

For my Noah.

ISBN: 978-1-941302-77-4

Library of Congress Control Number: 2018932759

www.lionforge.com

10 9 8 7 6 5 4 3 2 1

OOTHAR
THE
BLUE

BRANDON REESE

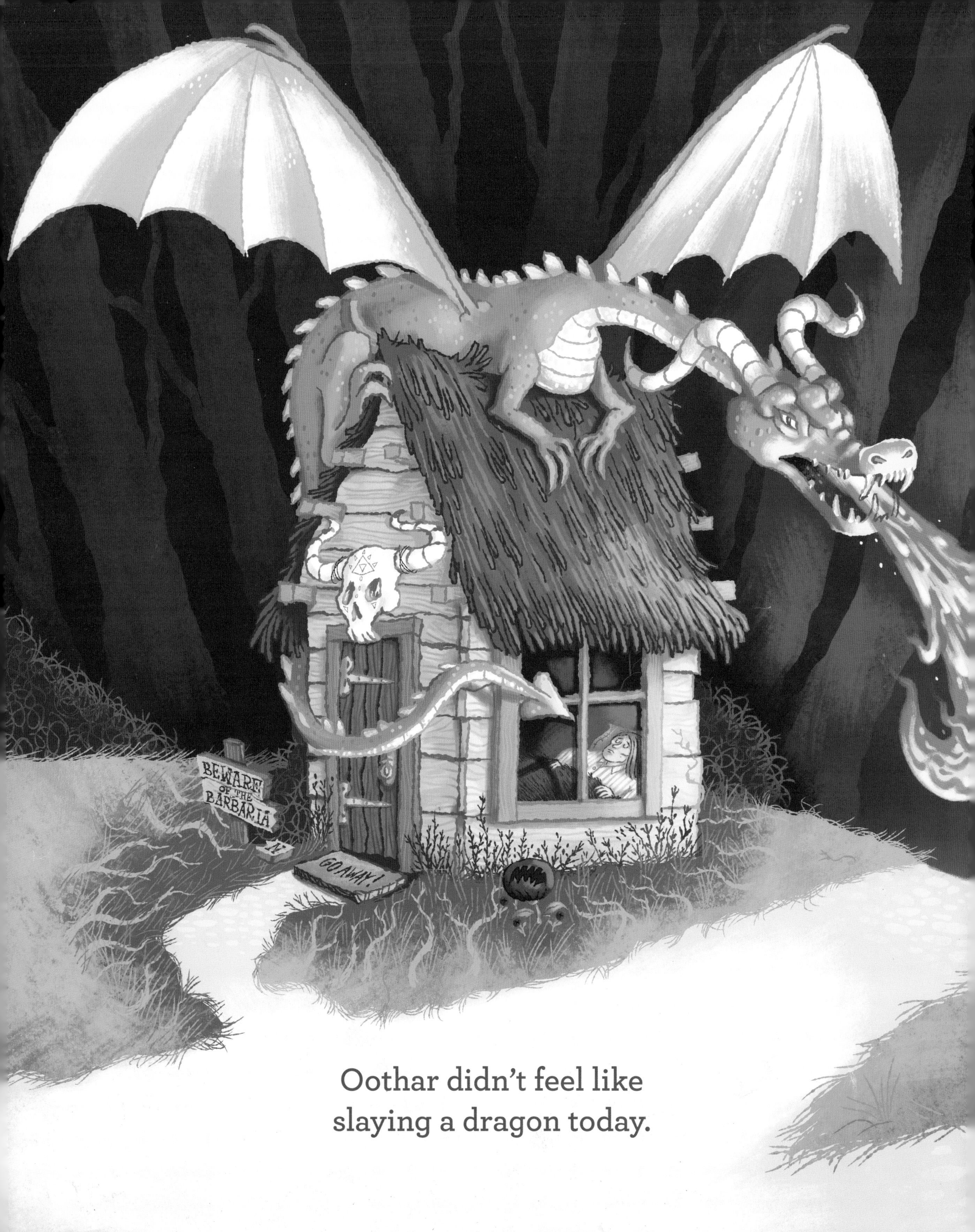
BEWARE
OF THE
BARBARIA
GO AWAY!

Oothar didn't feel like
slaying a dragon today.

He didn't feel like smashing
an ogre's heads together either.

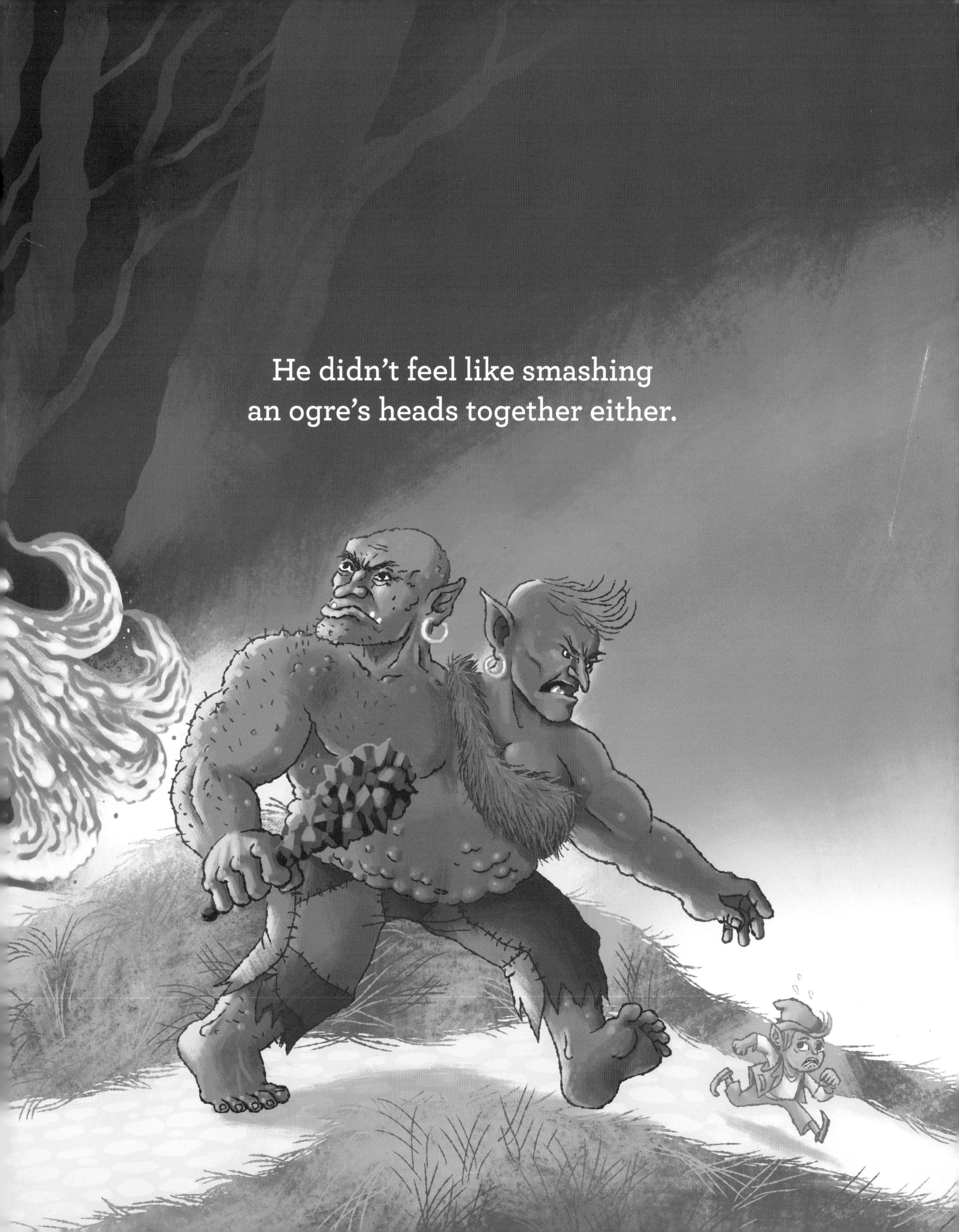

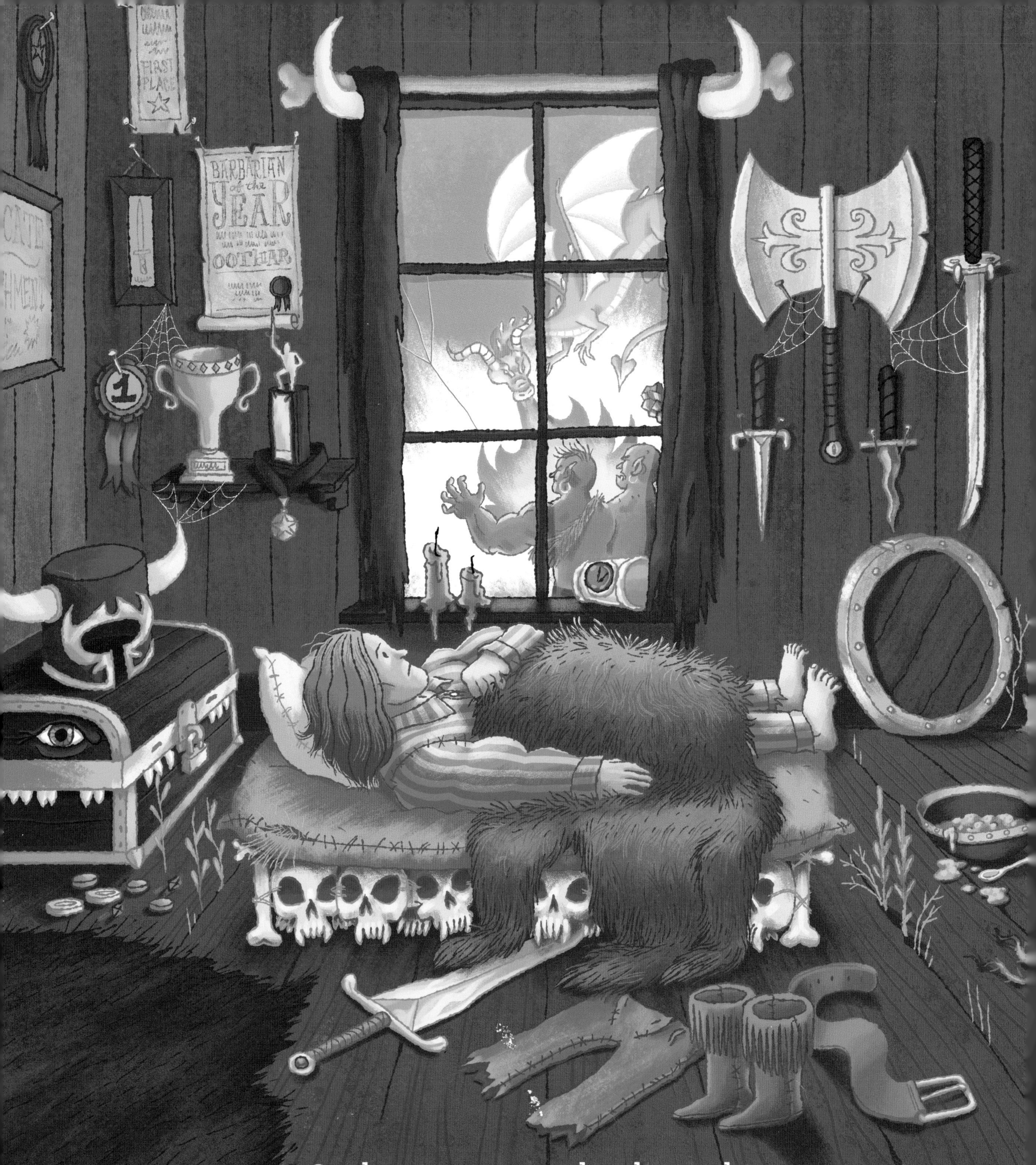
FIRST PLACE
BARBARIAN of the YEAR
OOTHAR
1

Oothar just wanted to lie on his
bed of bugbear bones and sleep the day away.

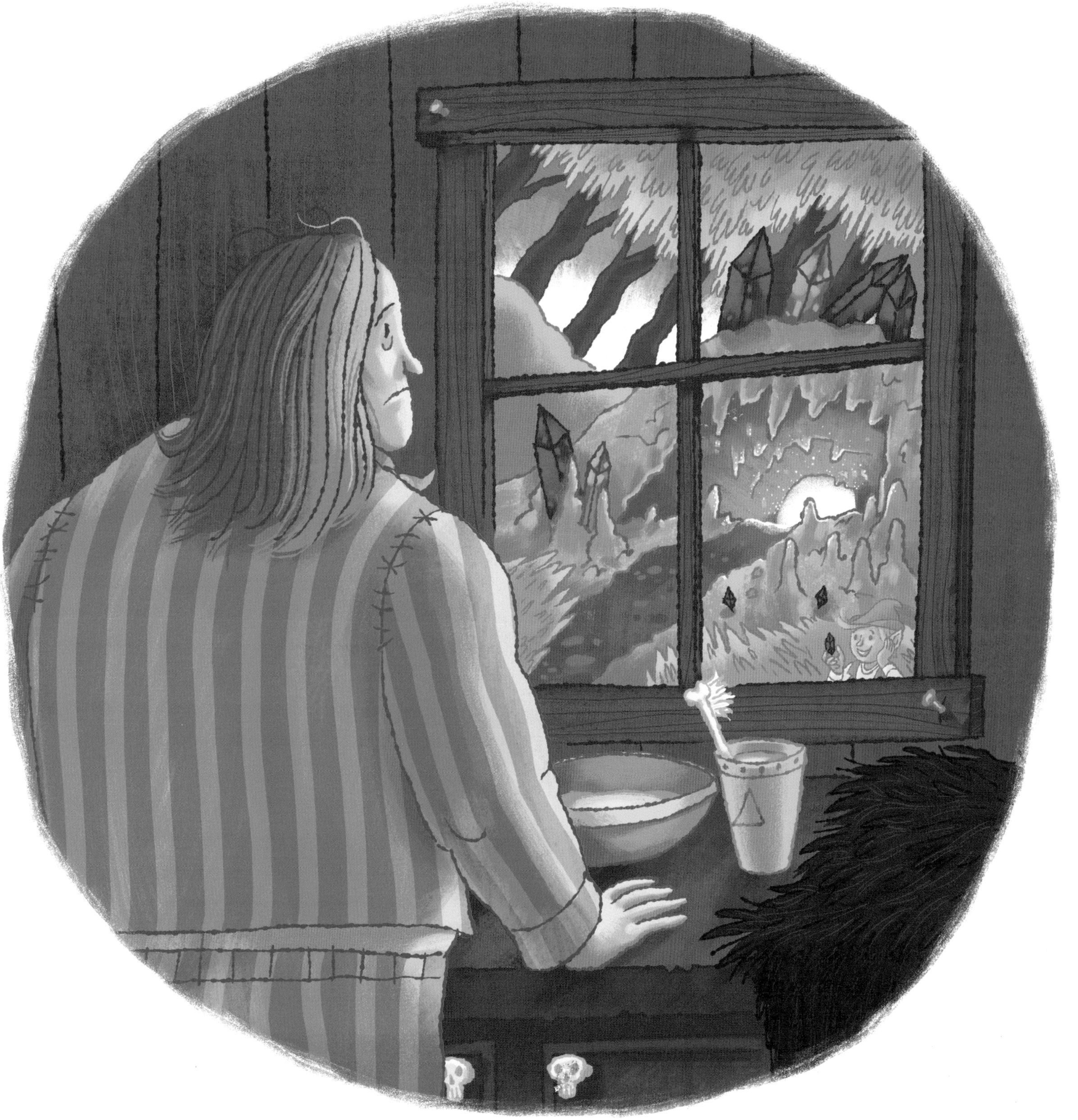

Pillaging the catacombs would have to wait.

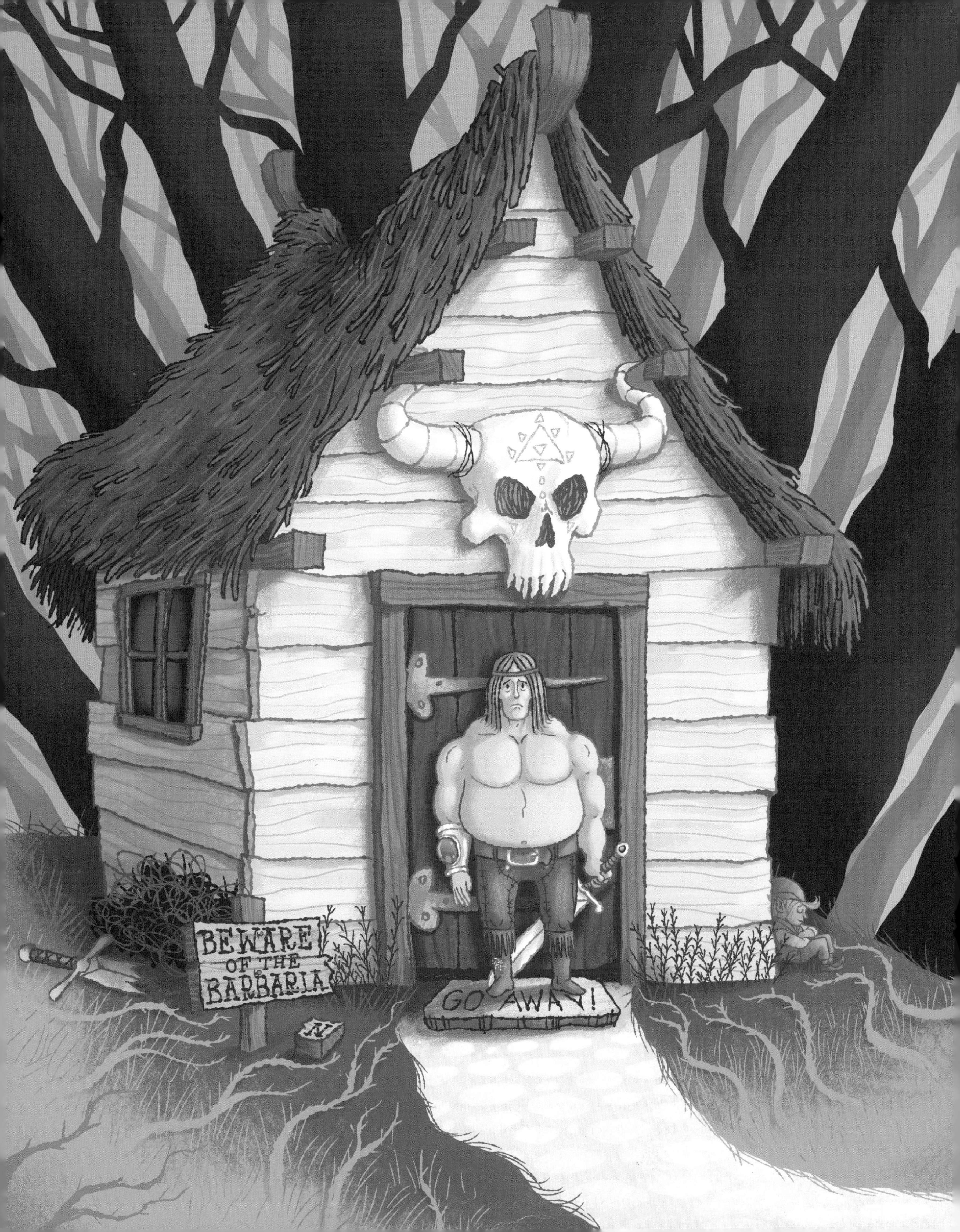
BEWARE OF THE BARBARIA
GO AWAY!

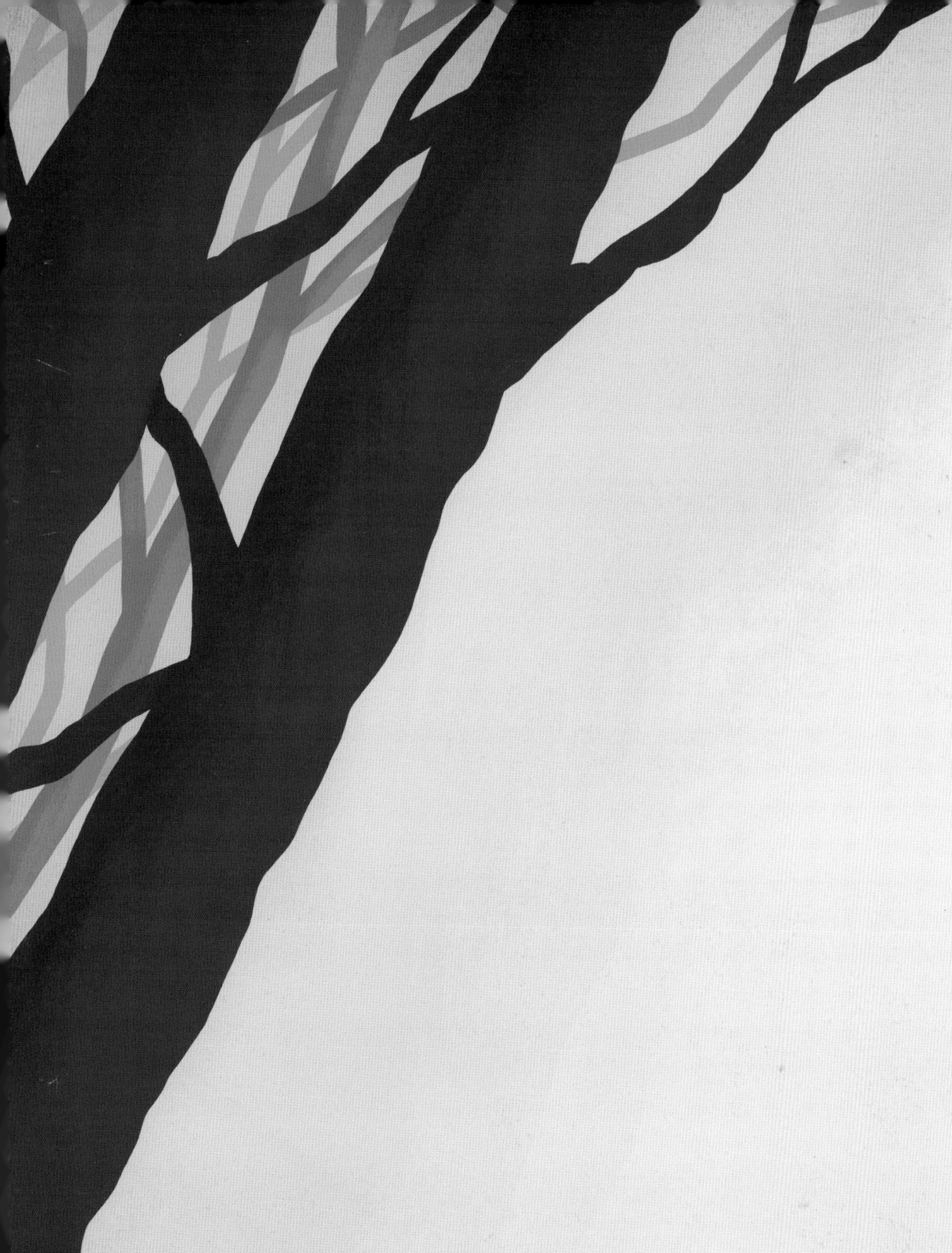

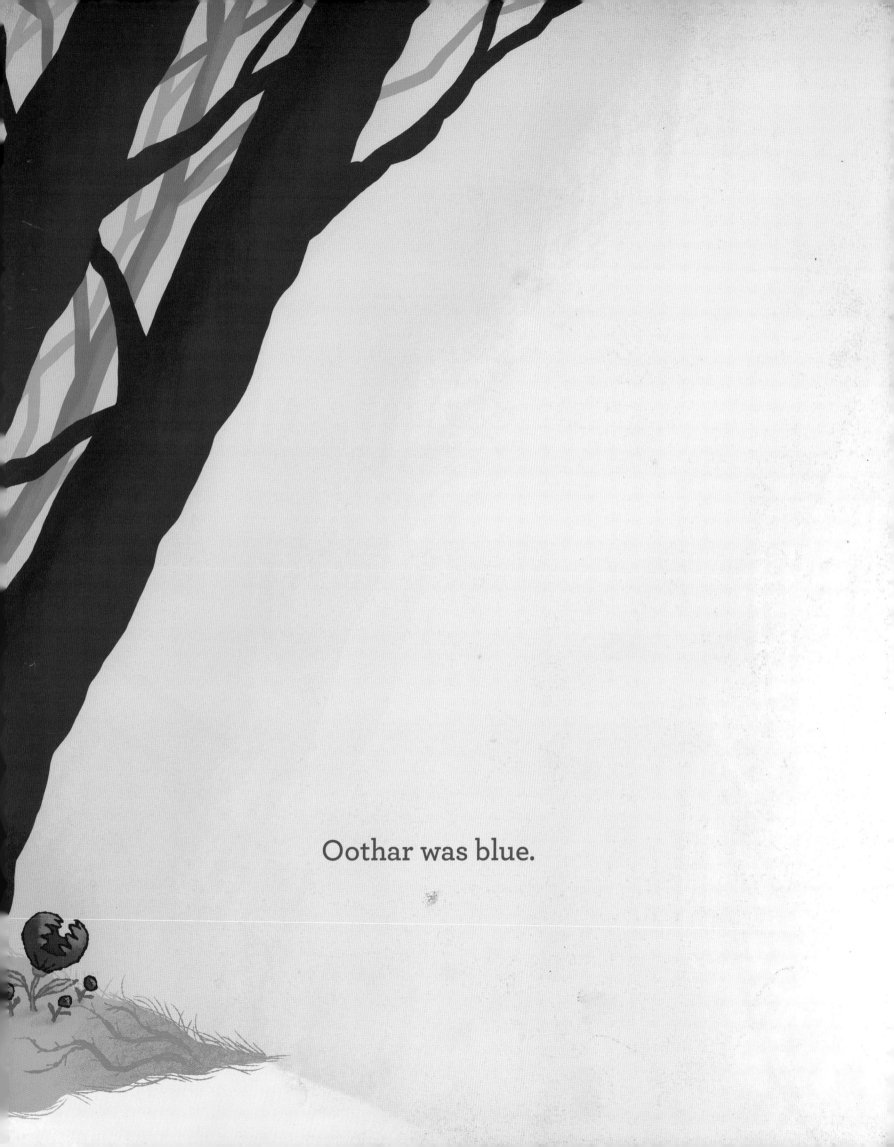

Oothar was blue.

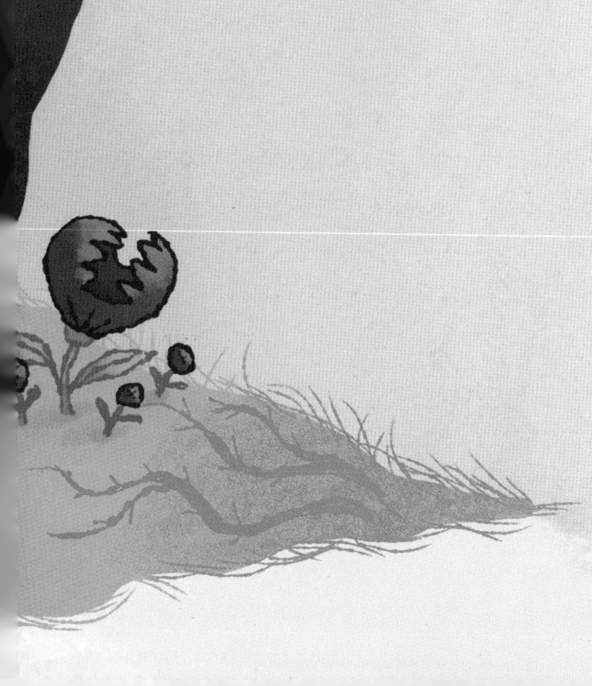

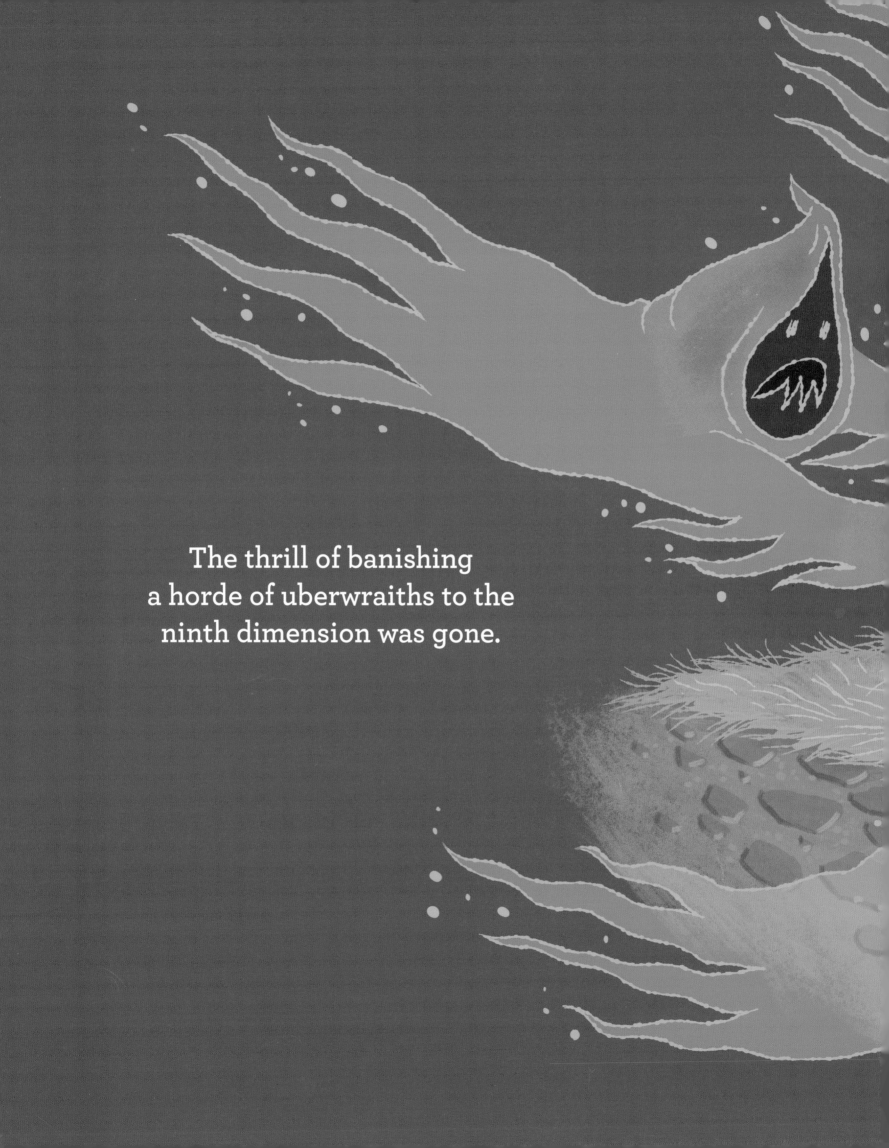

The thrill of banishing
a horde of uberwraiths to the
ninth dimension was gone.

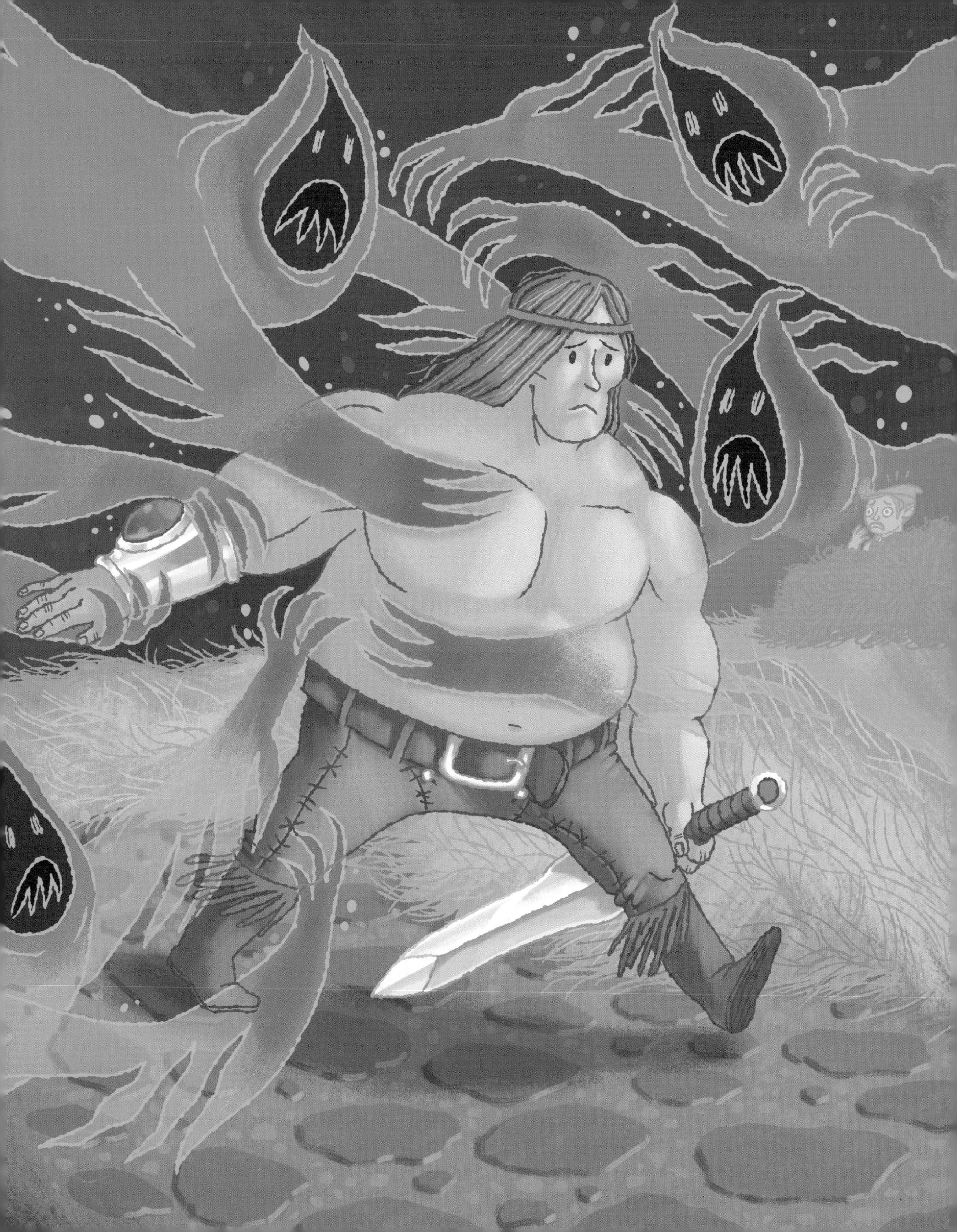

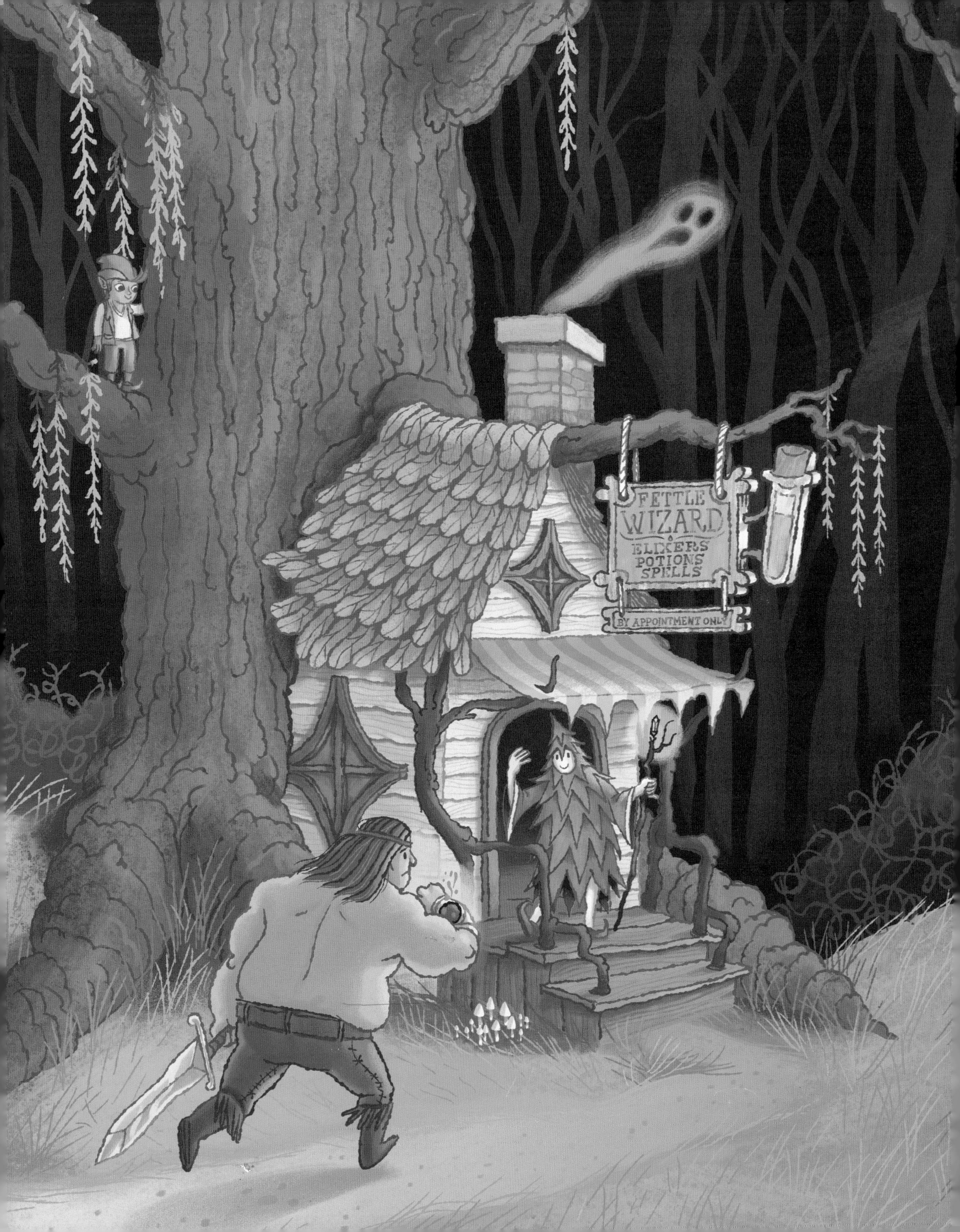
FETTLE
WIZARD
ELIXERS
POTIONS
SPELLS
BY APPOINTMENT ONLY

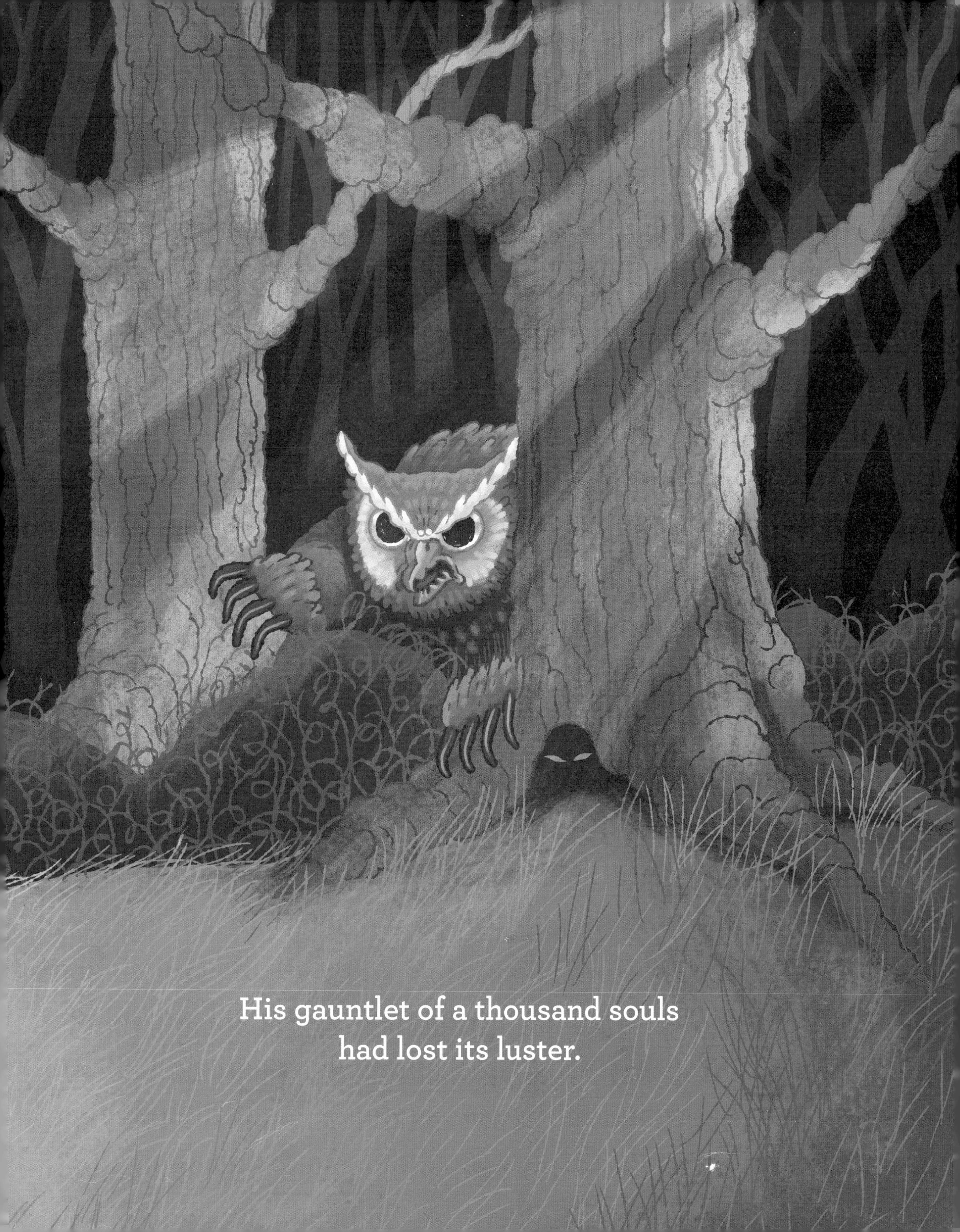

His gauntlet of a thousand souls
had lost its luster.

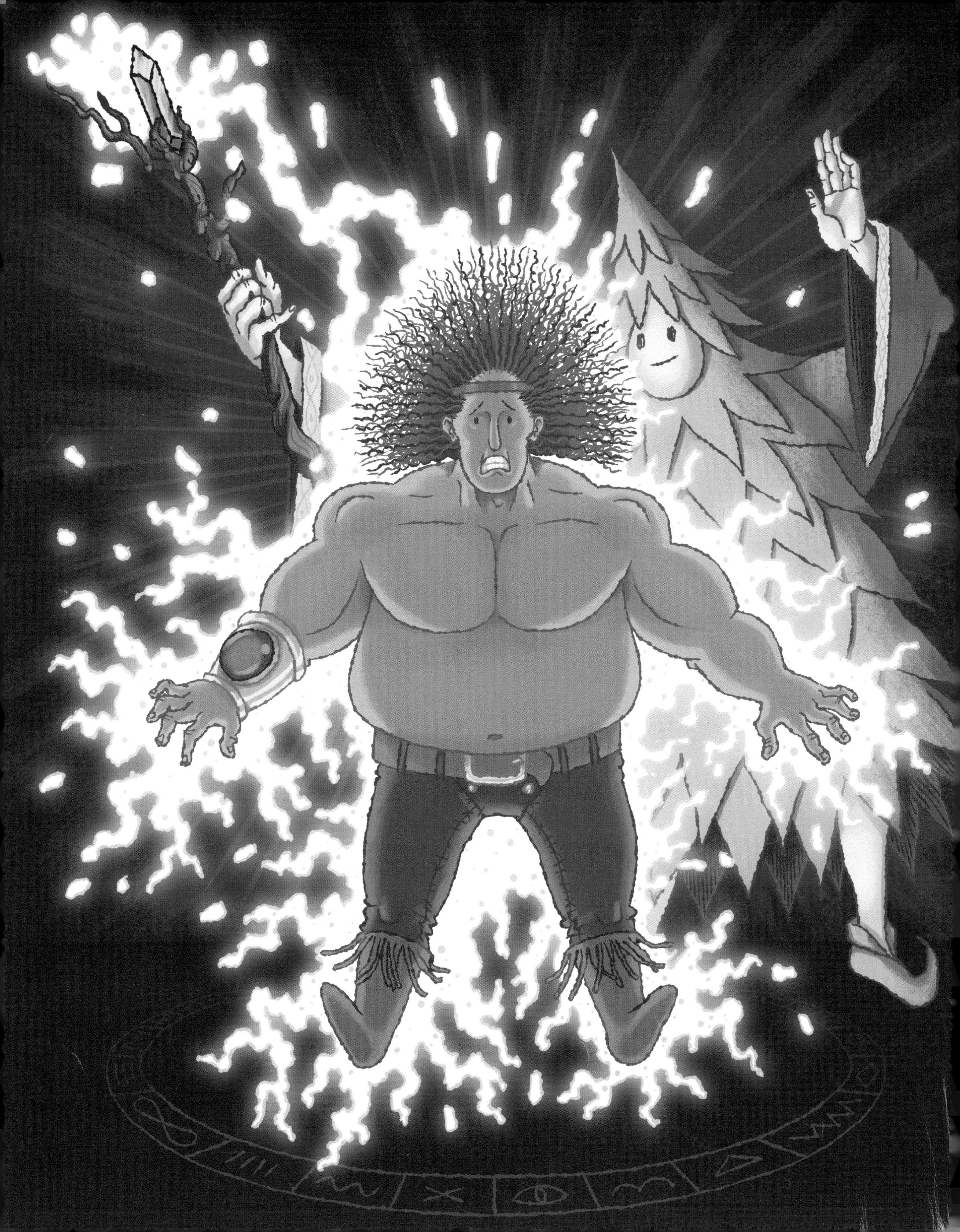

The Fettle Wizard's spell of enchantment
failed to bring him any relief.

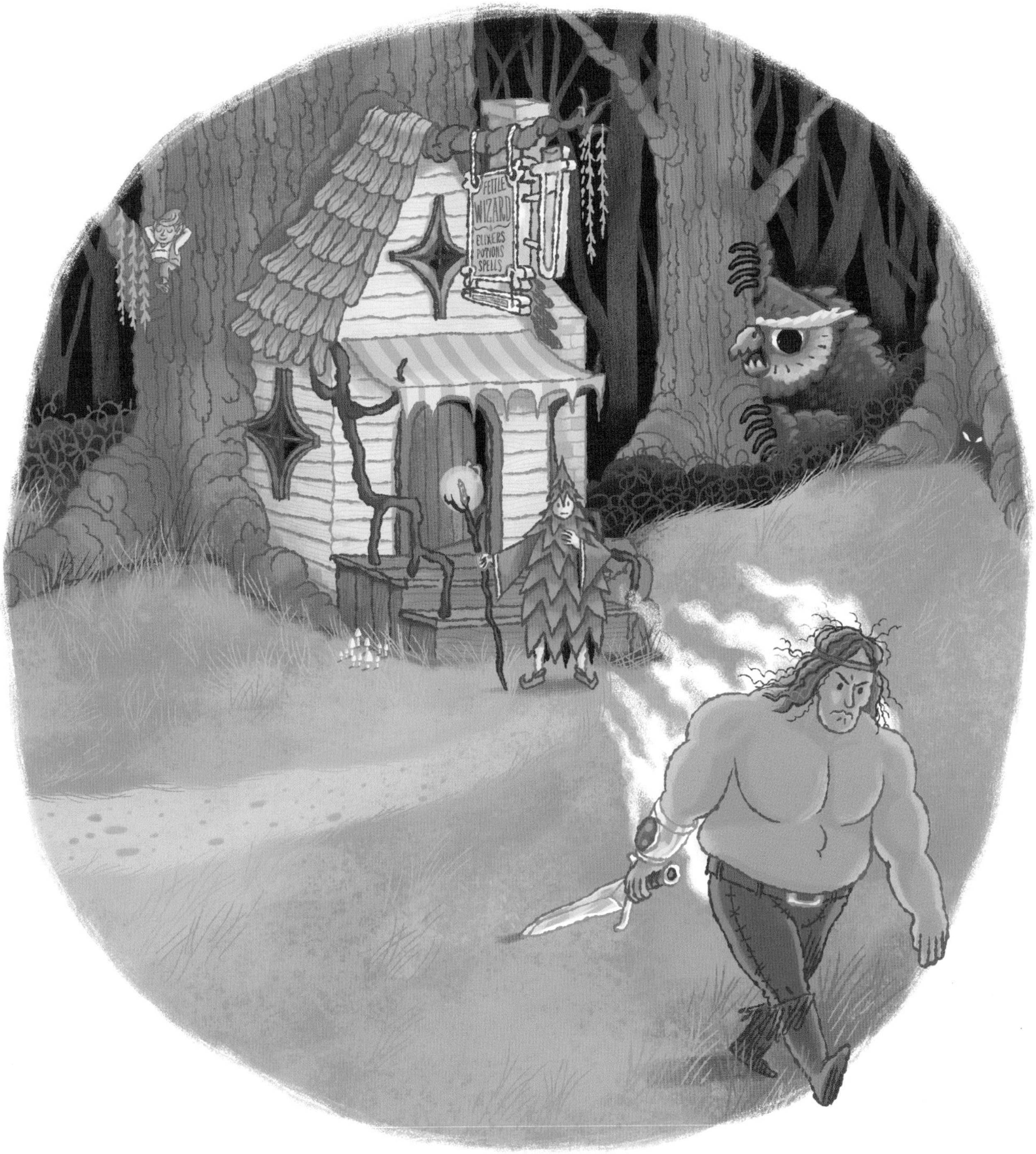
FETTLE WIZARD
ELIXERS
POTIONS
SPELLS

Poor Oothar.

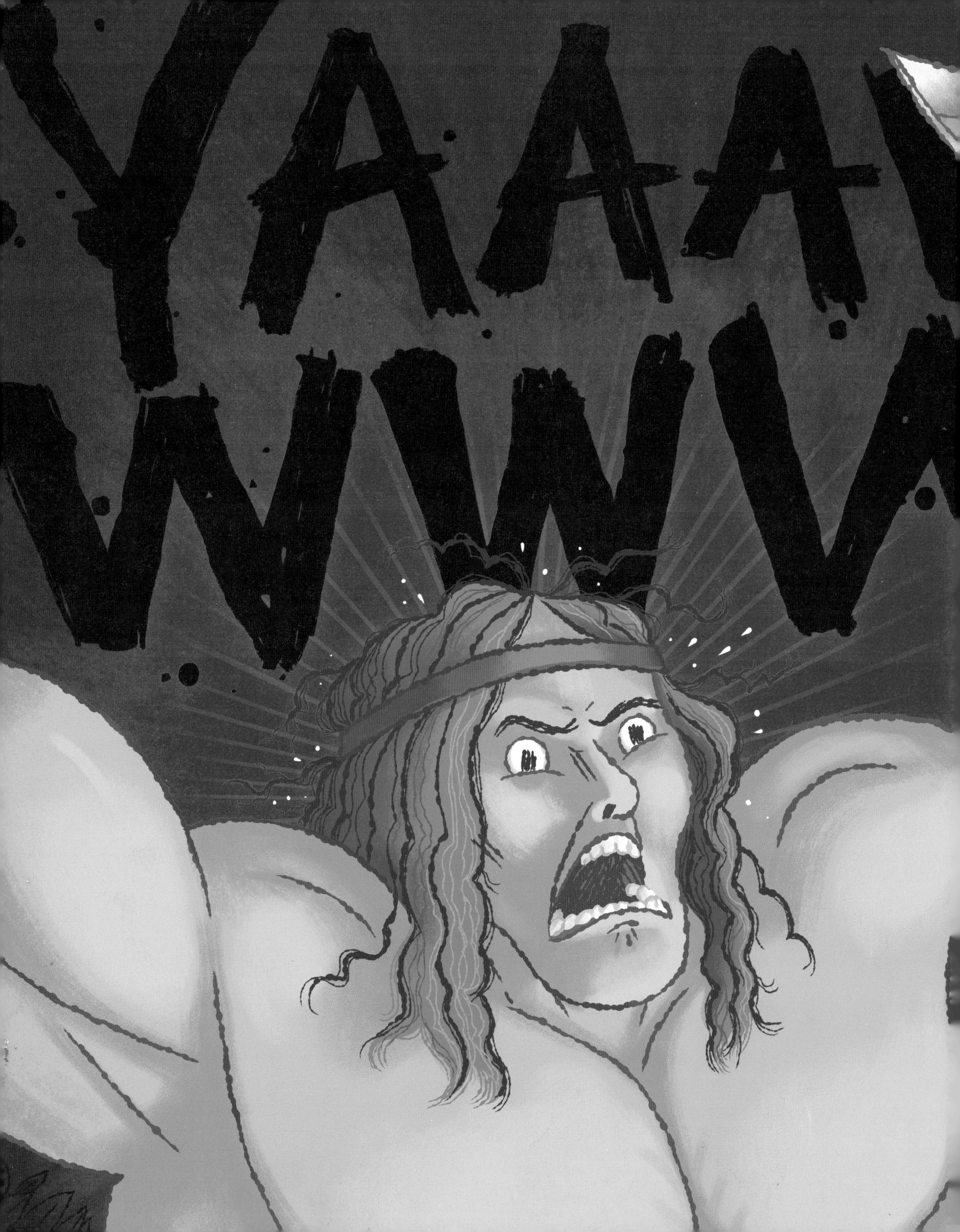
YAAA
WWW

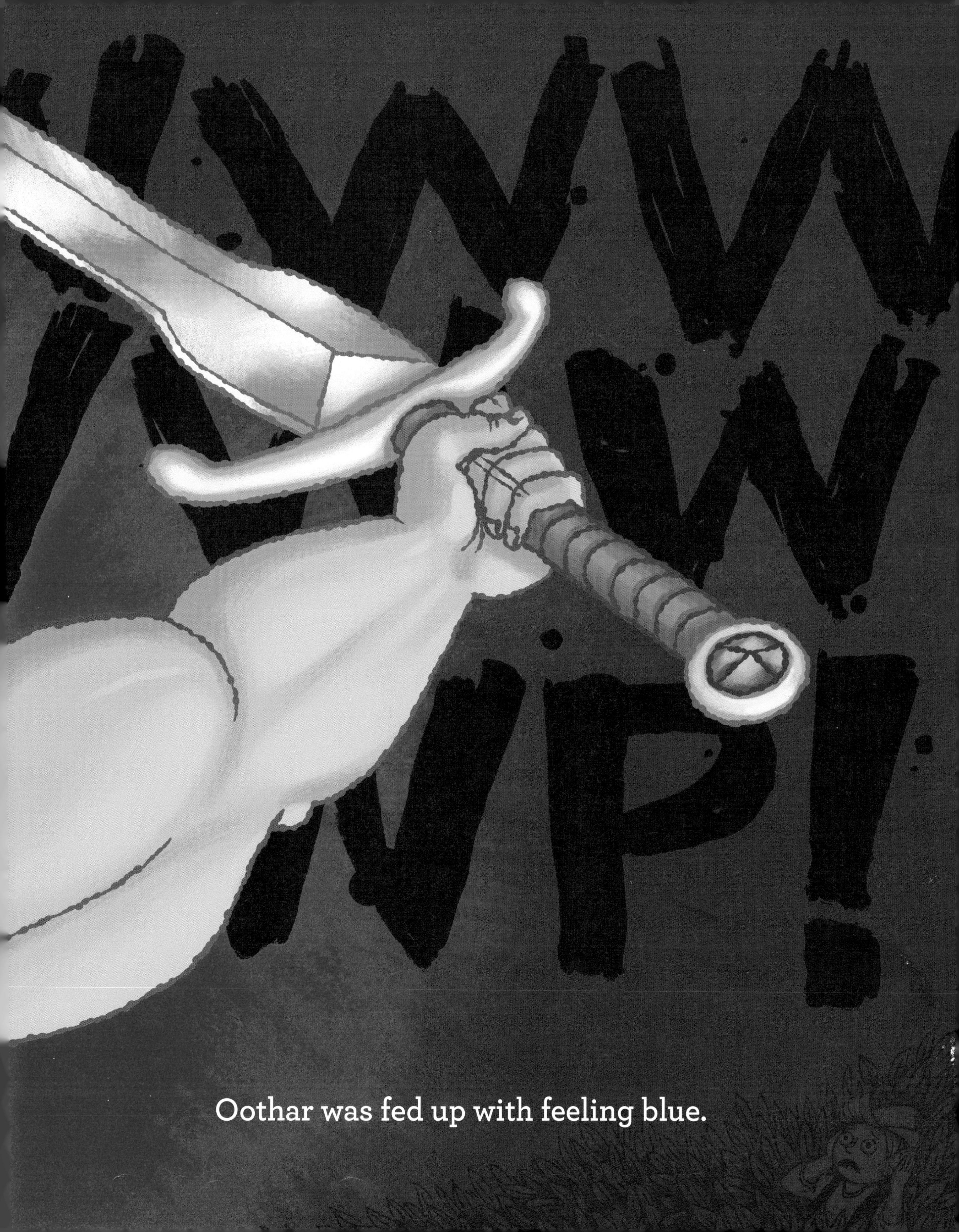

Oothar was fed up with feeling blue.

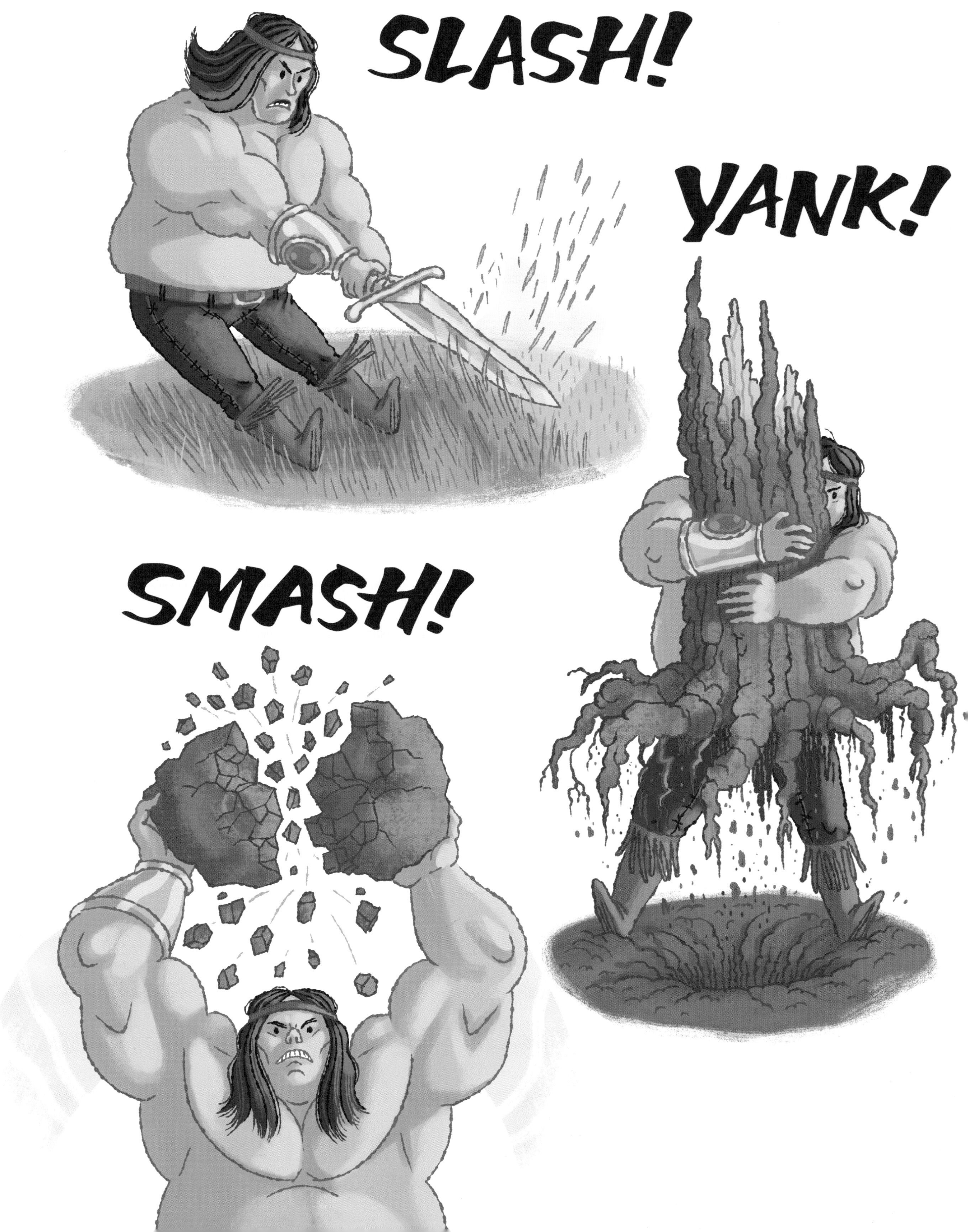
SLASH!
YANK!
SMASH!

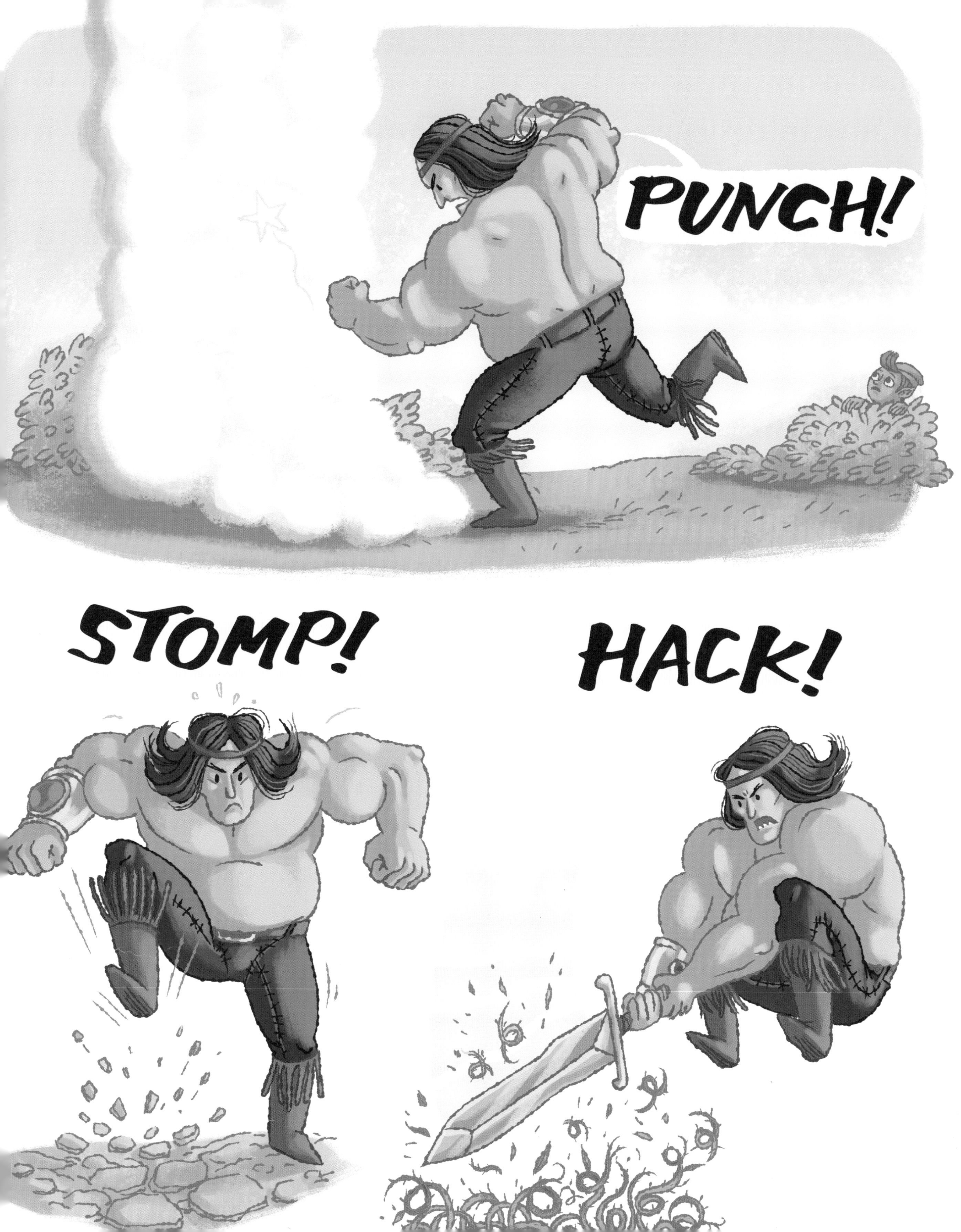
PUNCH!
STOMP!
HACK!

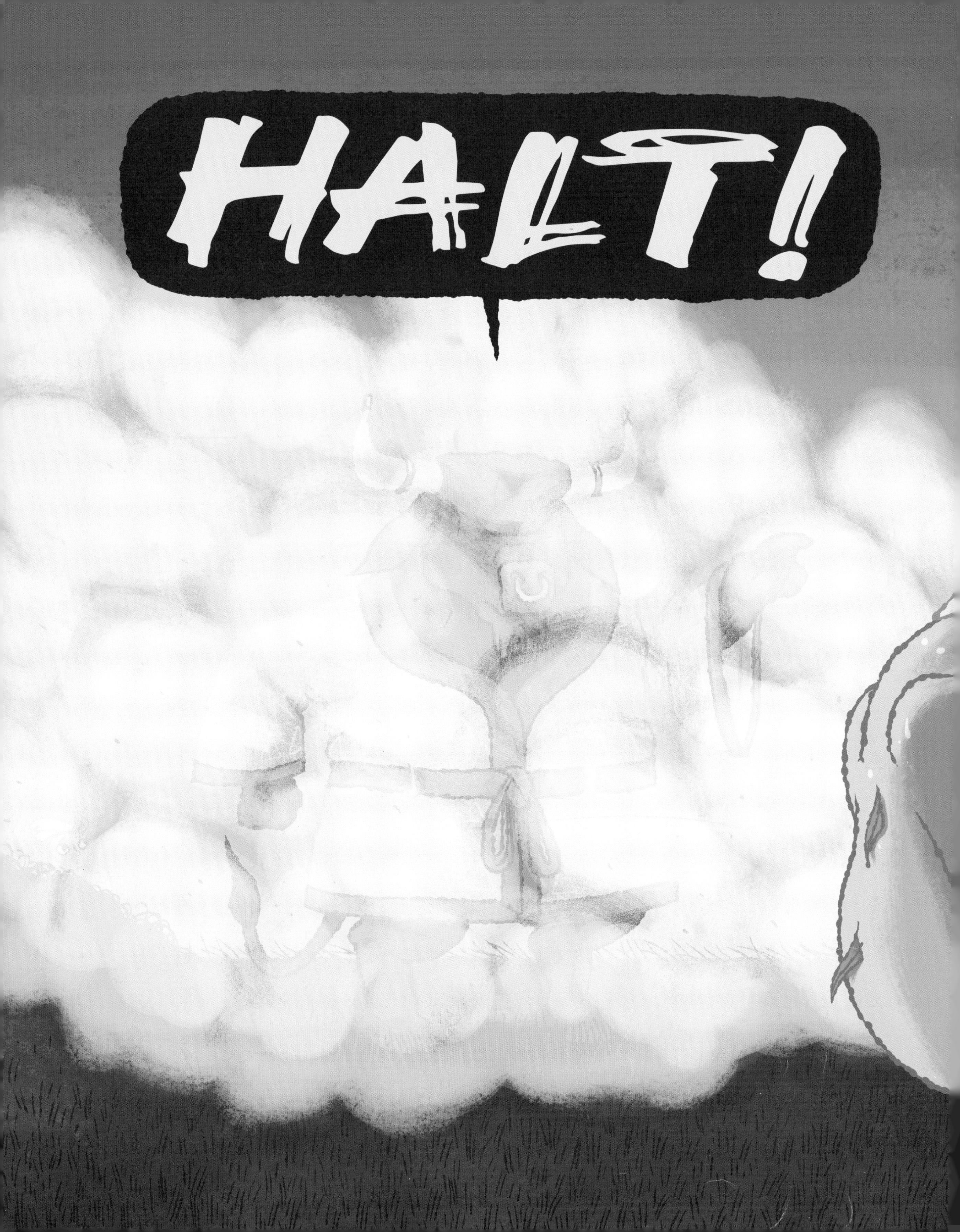
HALT!

“Who dares challenge me?”
asked Oothar.

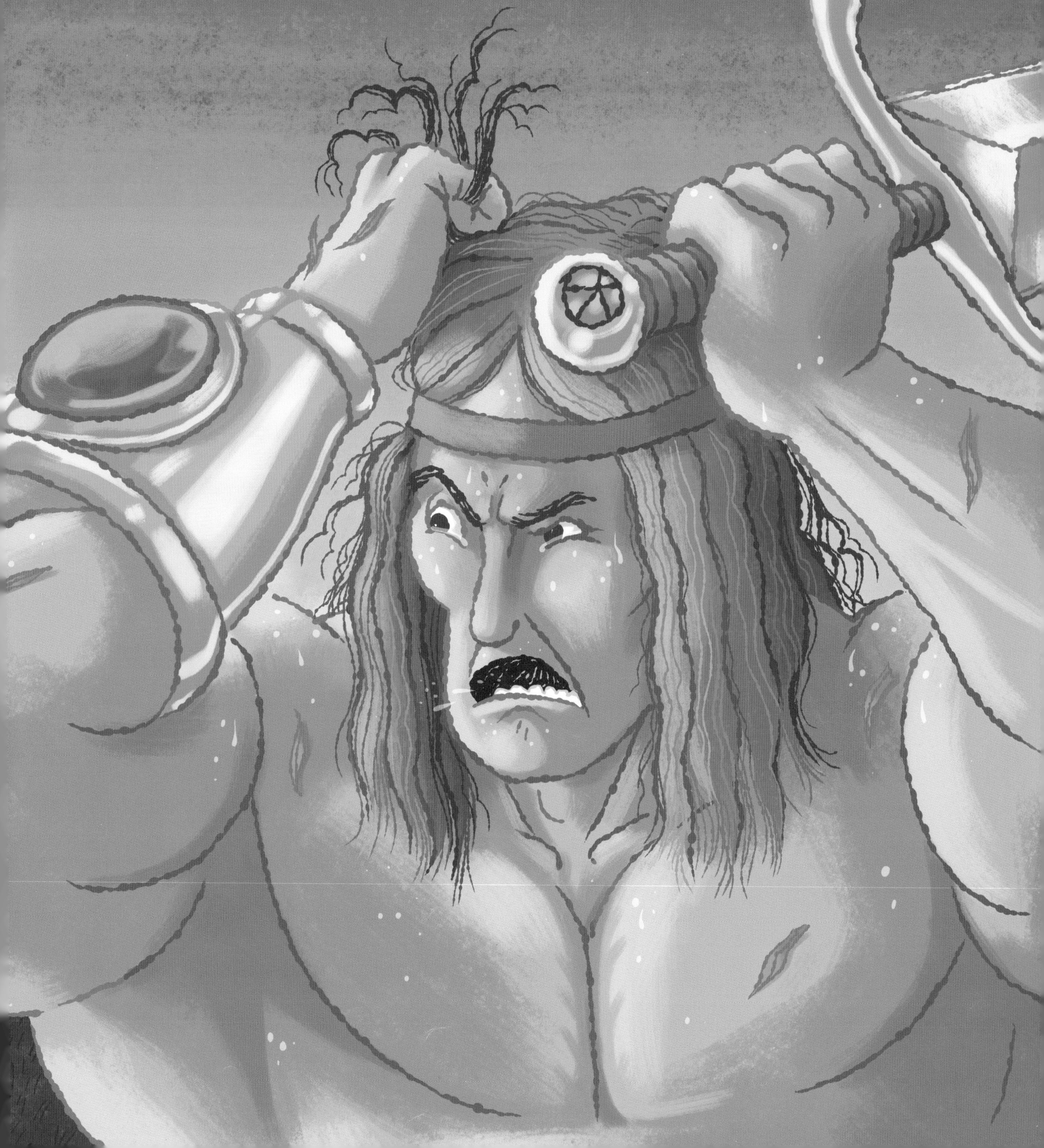

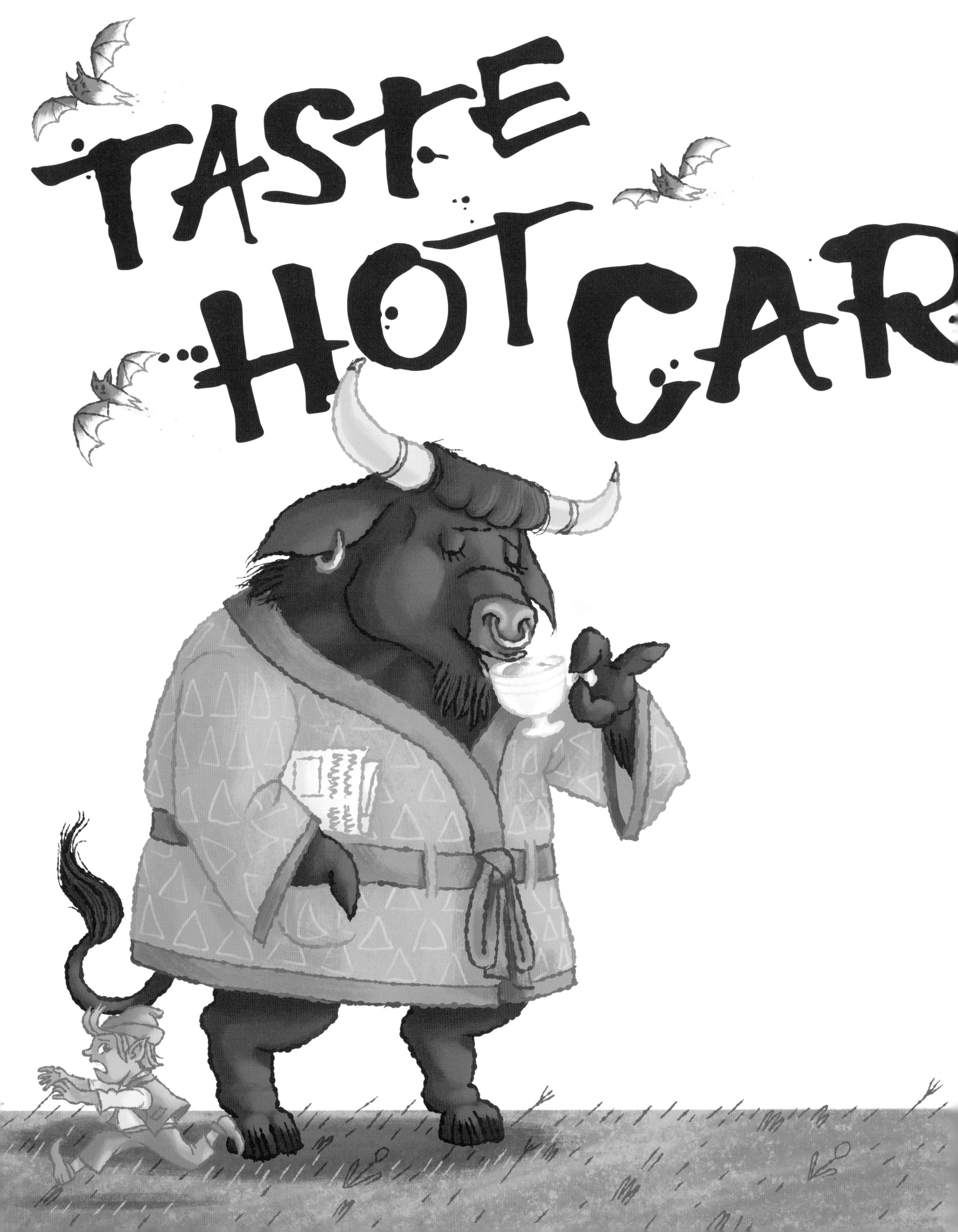
TASTE
HOT CAR

POOTHIAN STEEL!

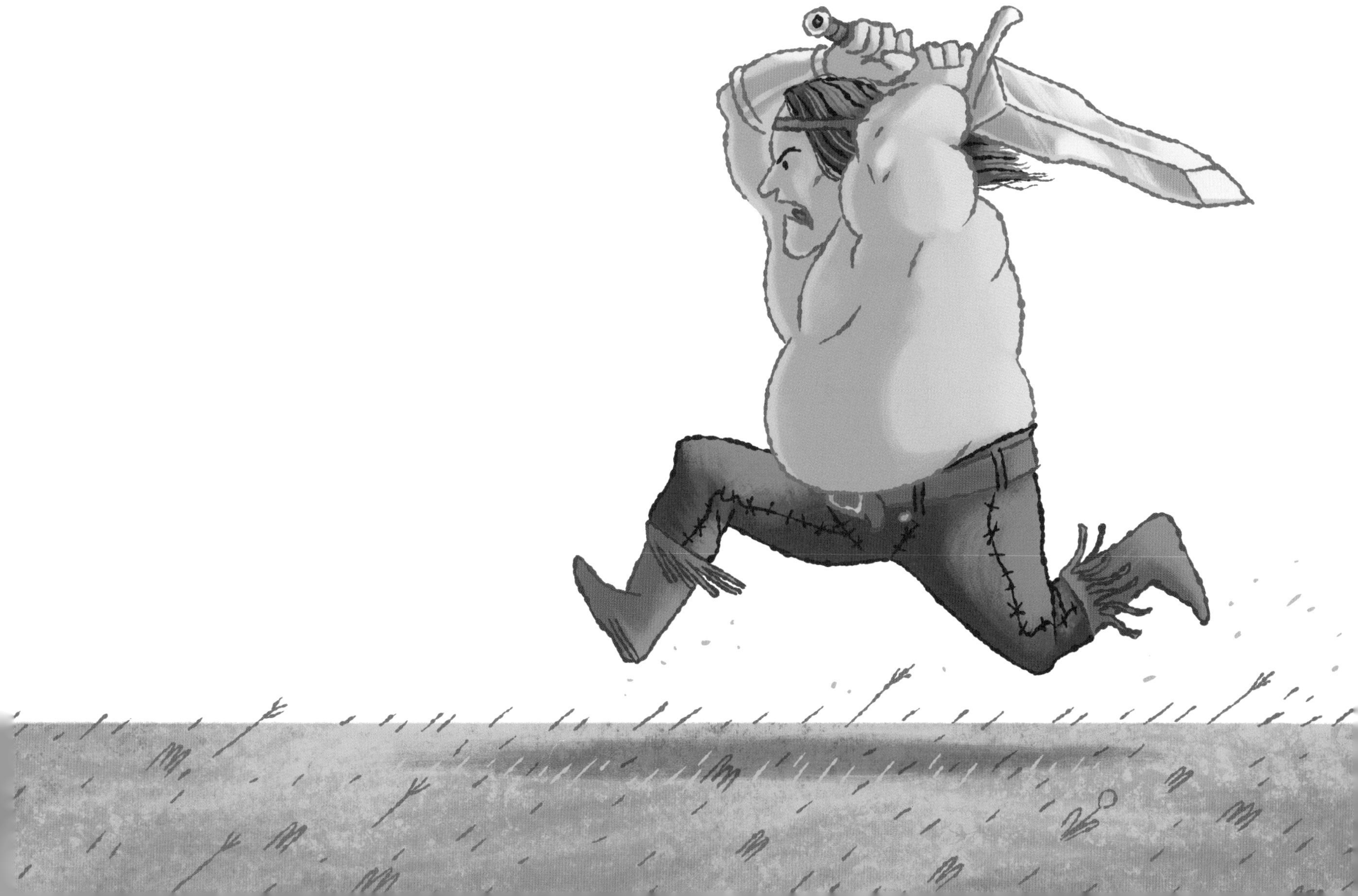

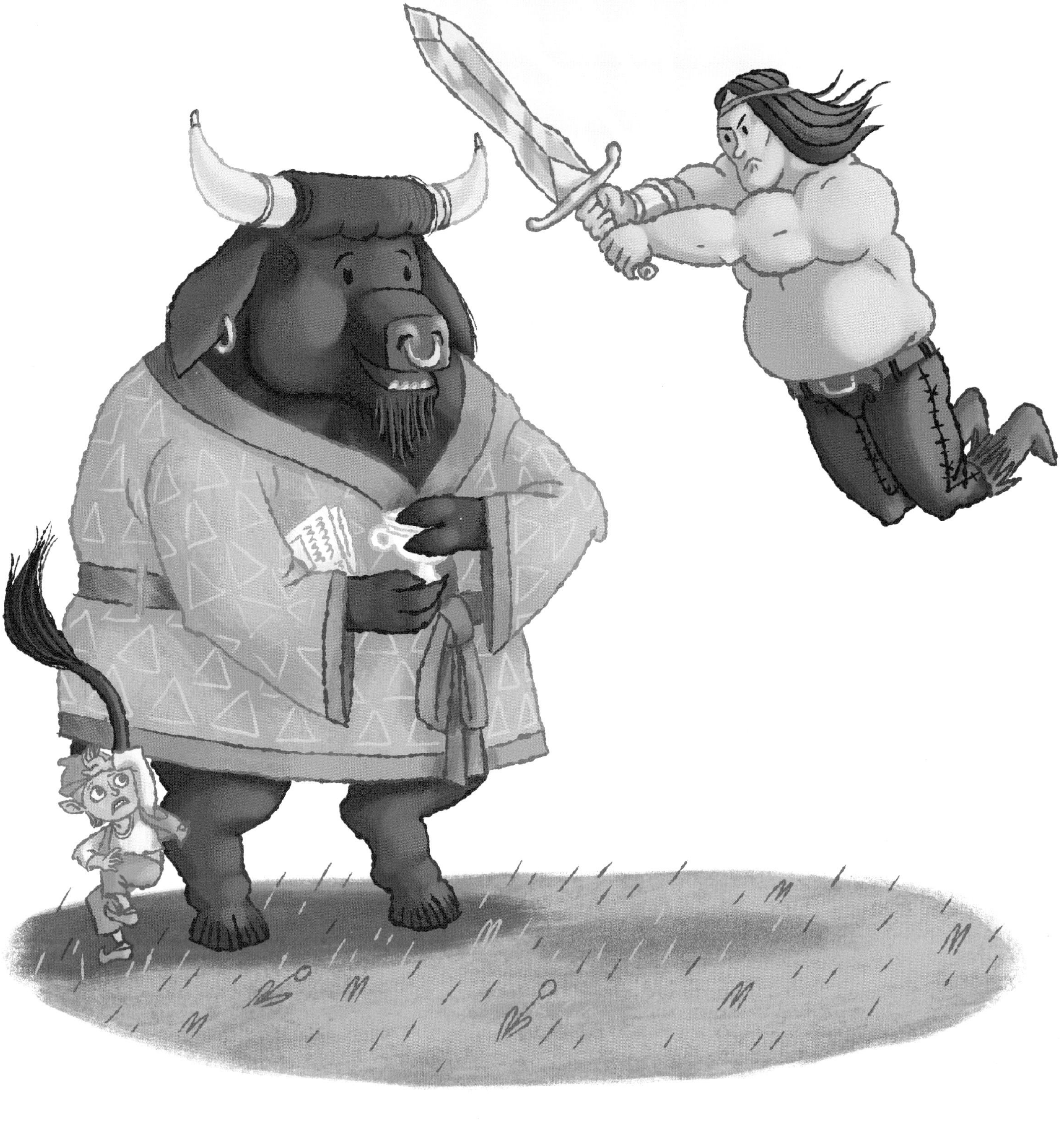

“Thank you!” said the minotaur.

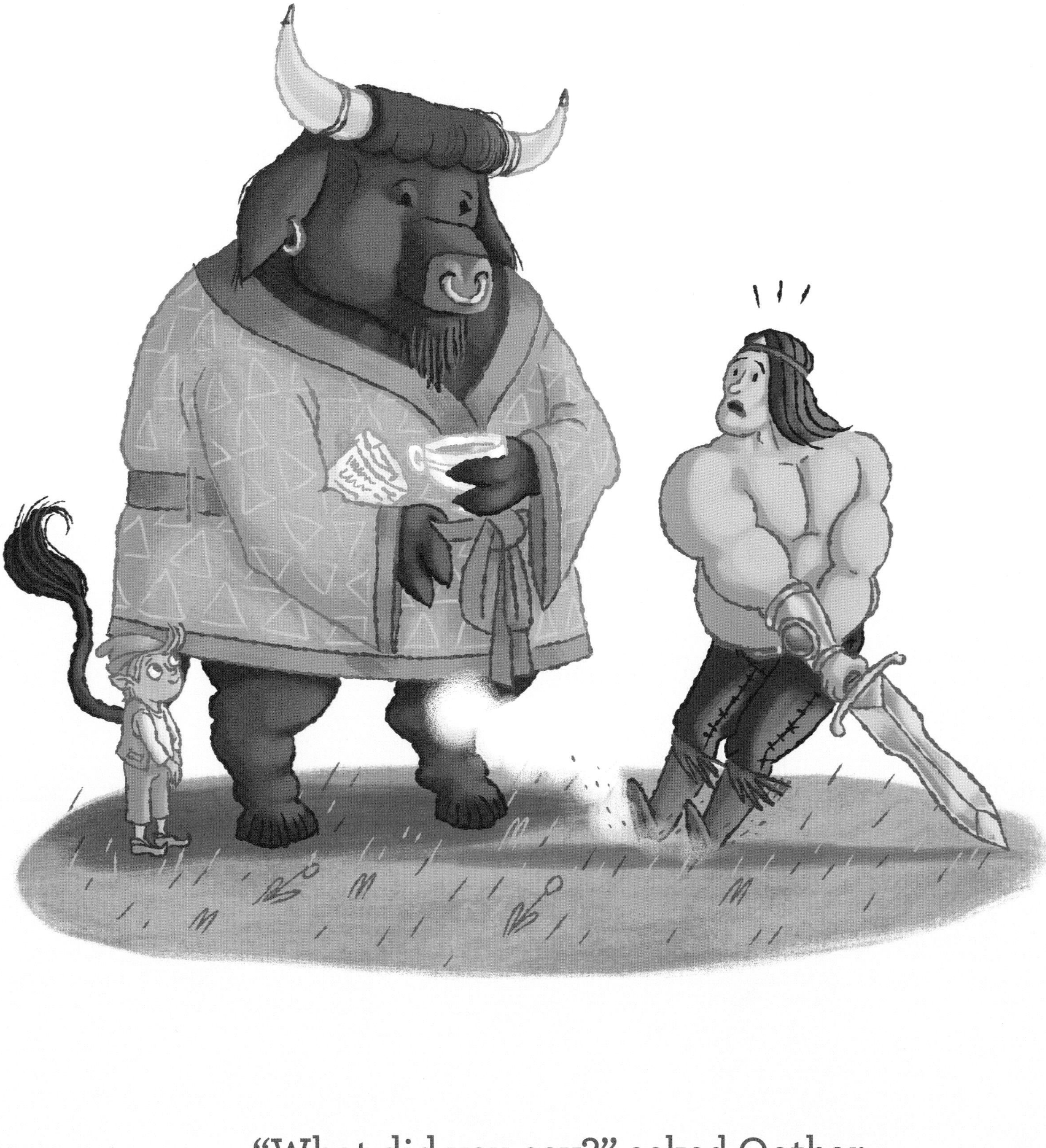

"What did you say?" asked Oothar.

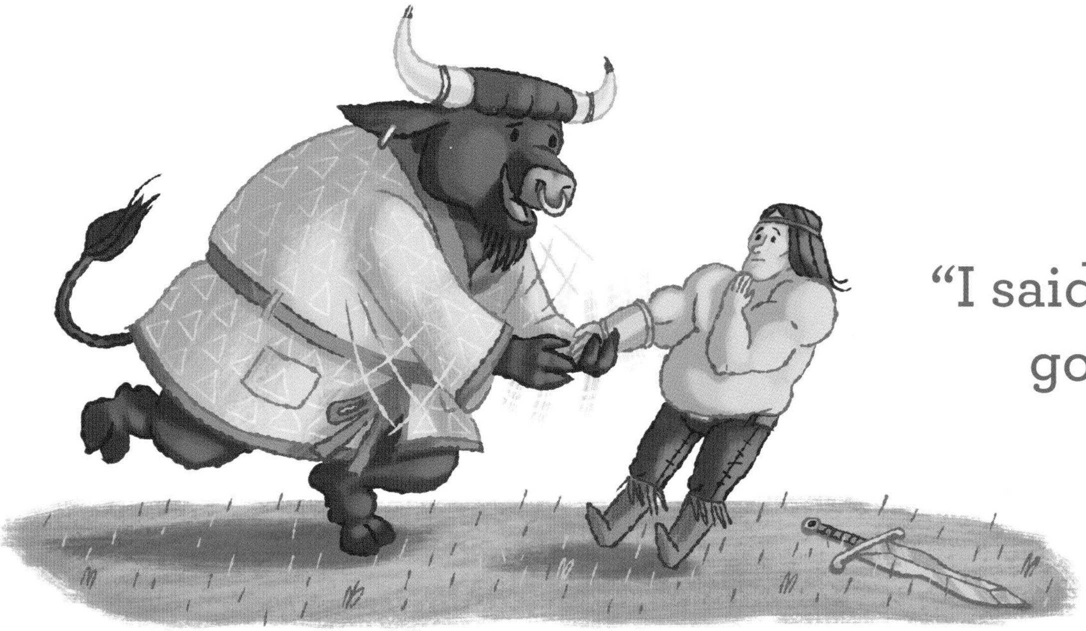

"I said thank you,
good sir!"

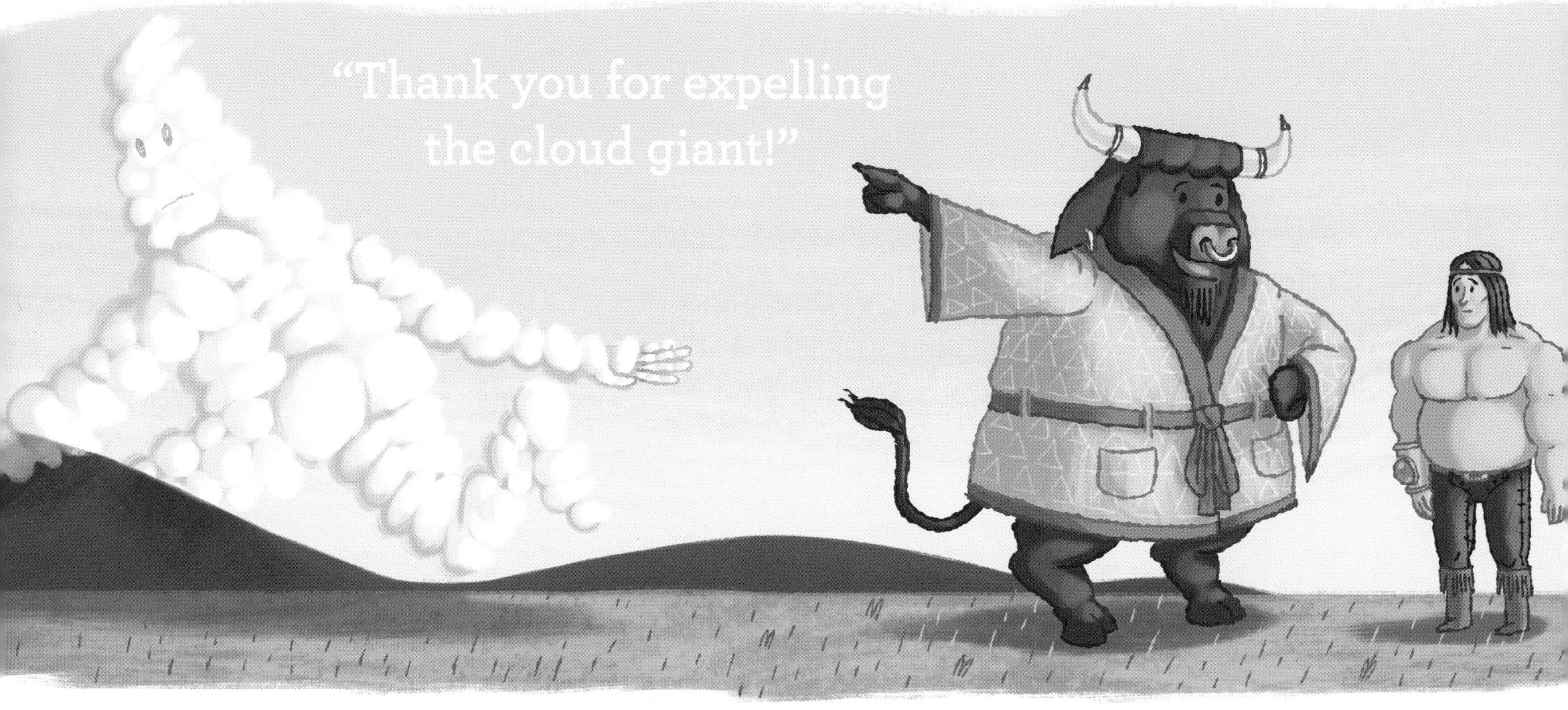
"Thank you for expelling
the cloud giant!"

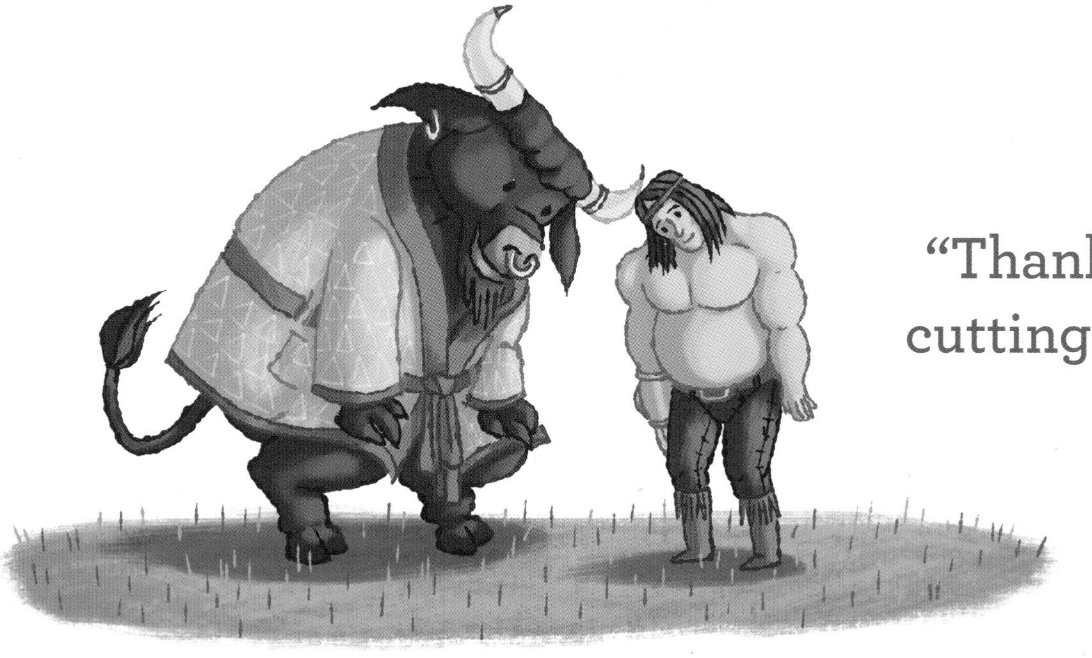

"Thank you for
cutting my grass!"

"Thank you for
trimming these bushes!"

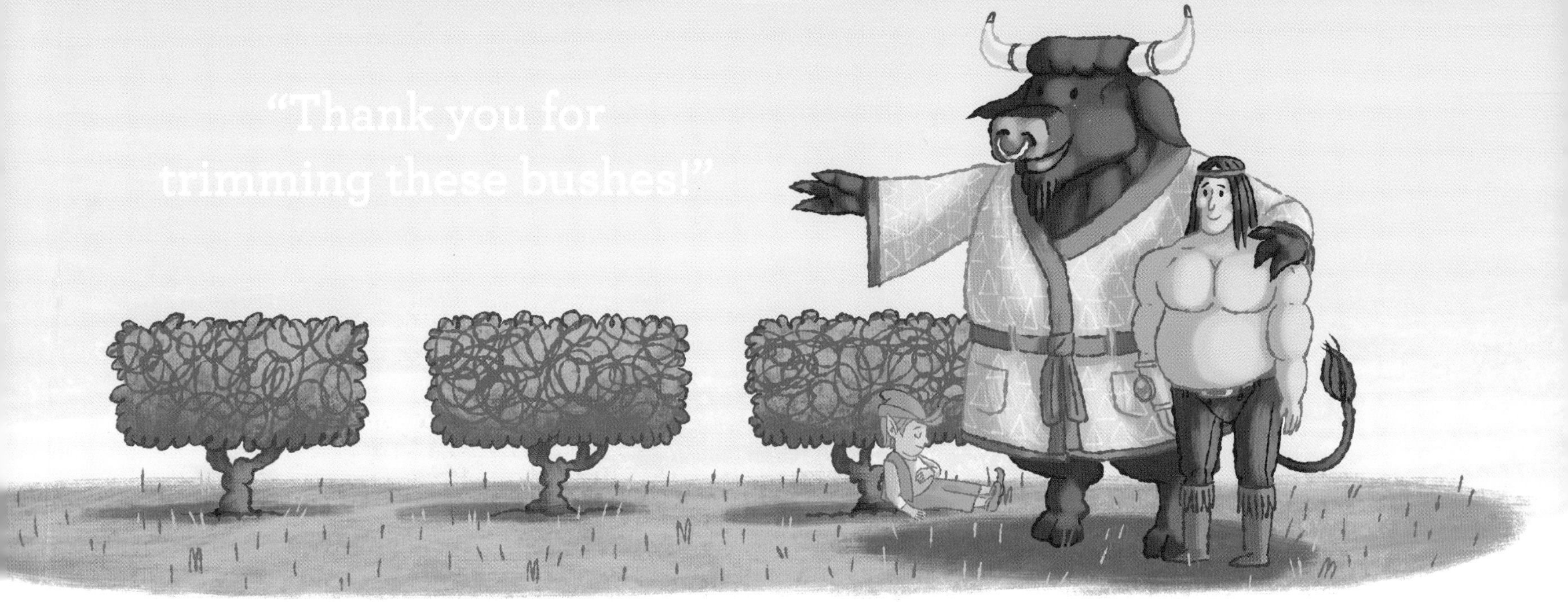

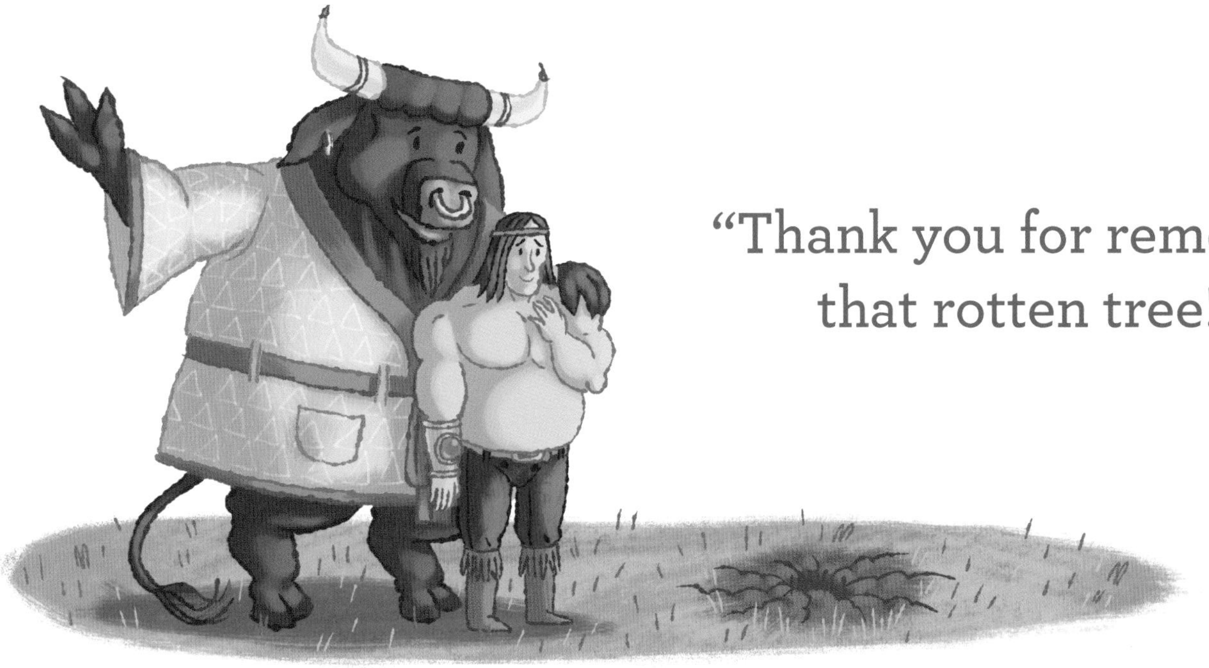

"Thank you for removing
that rotten tree!"

"And thank you for
creating this
stunning walkway!"

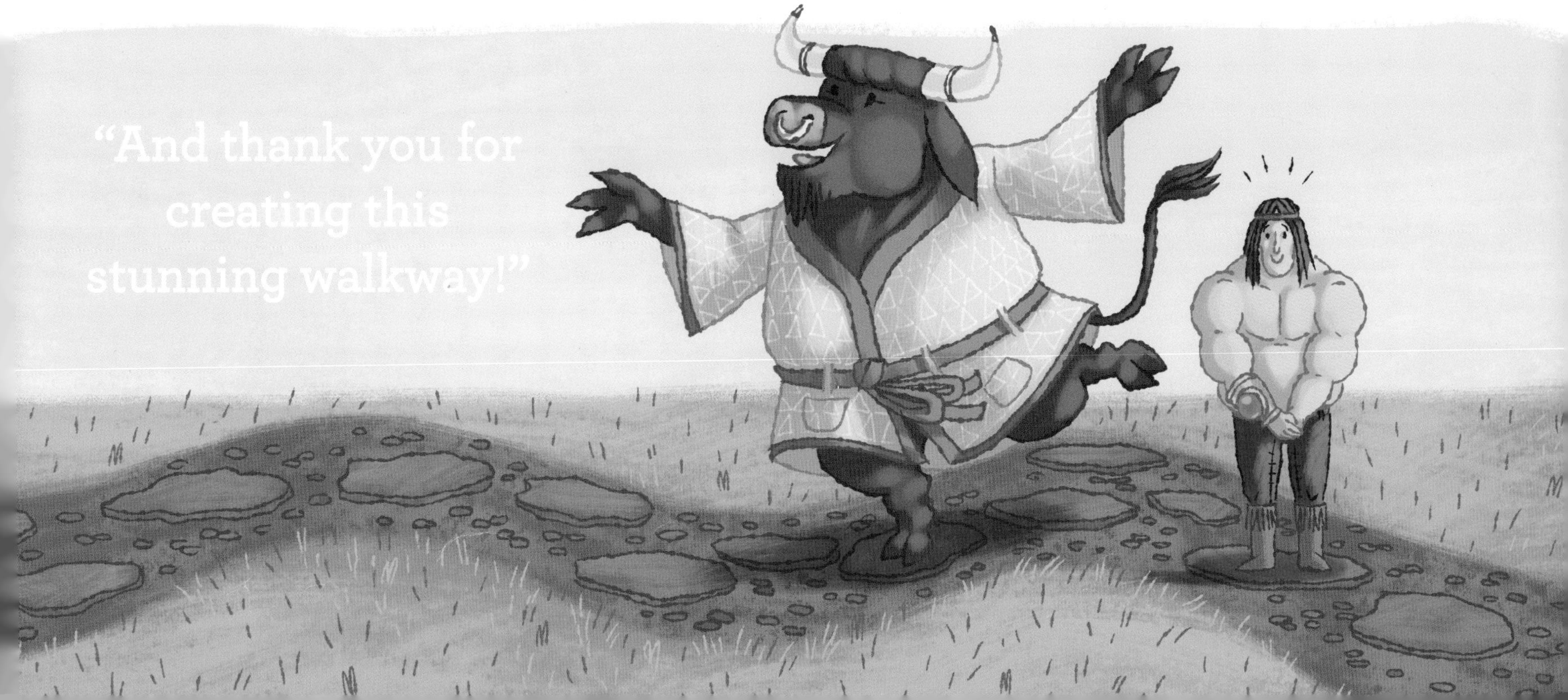

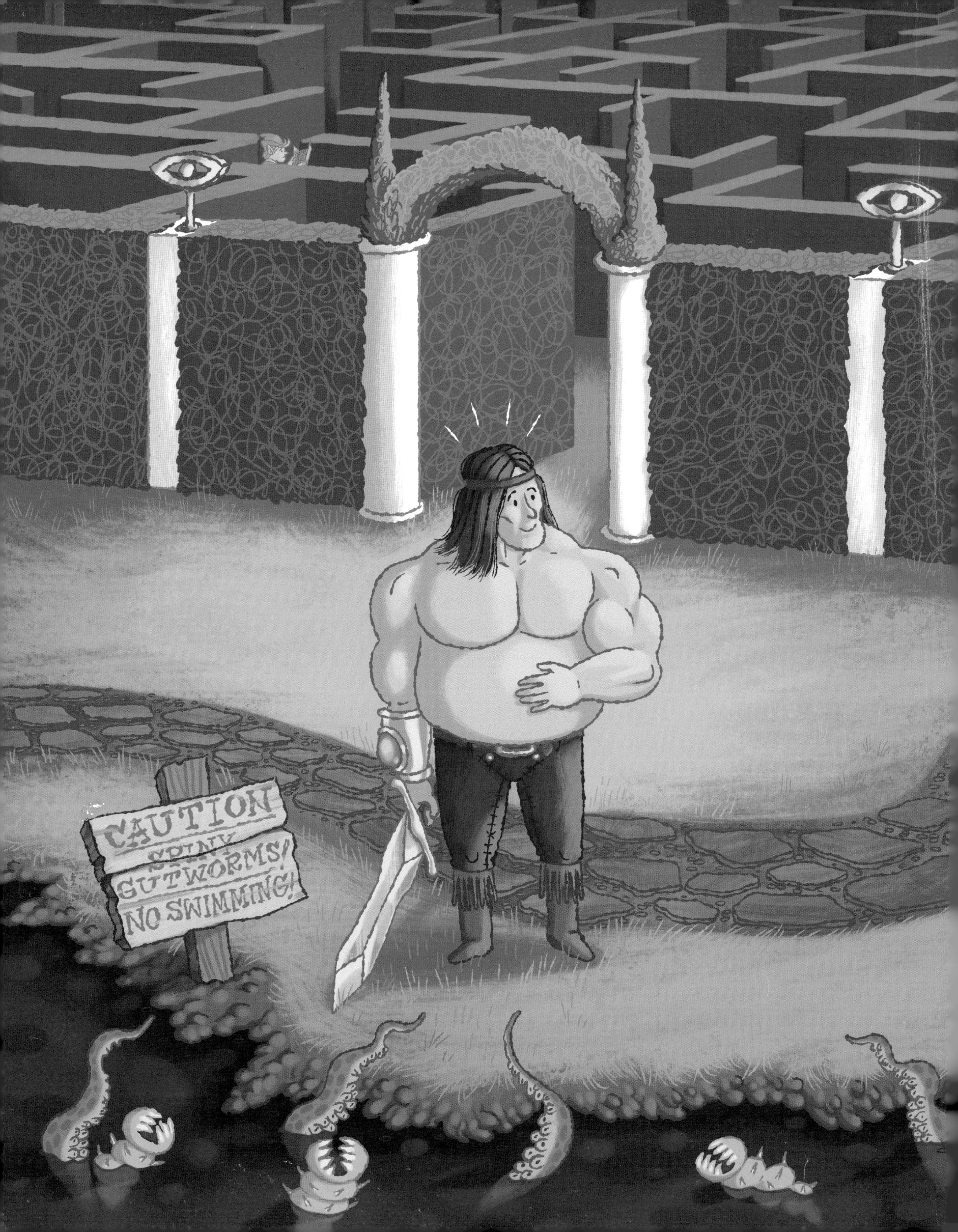
CAUTION
SPINY
GUTWORMS!
NO SWIMMING!

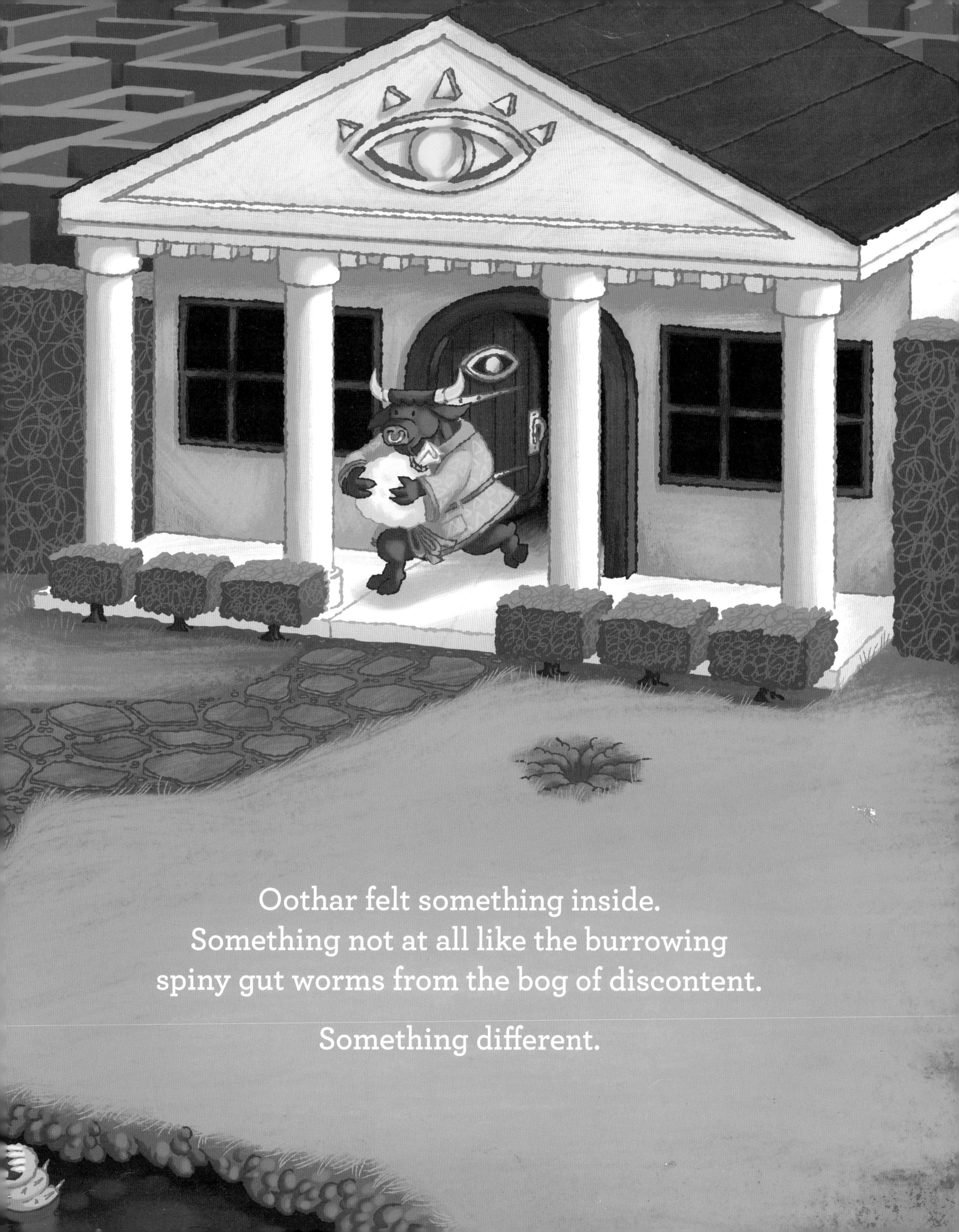

Oothar felt something inside.
Something not at all like the burrowing
spiny gut worms from the bog of discontent.

Something different.

"Please take this massive sack of gold coins in gratitude for your services!" said the minotaur.

"Do you have a card? No matter. I'm telling all my friends about Oothar the Landscaper!"

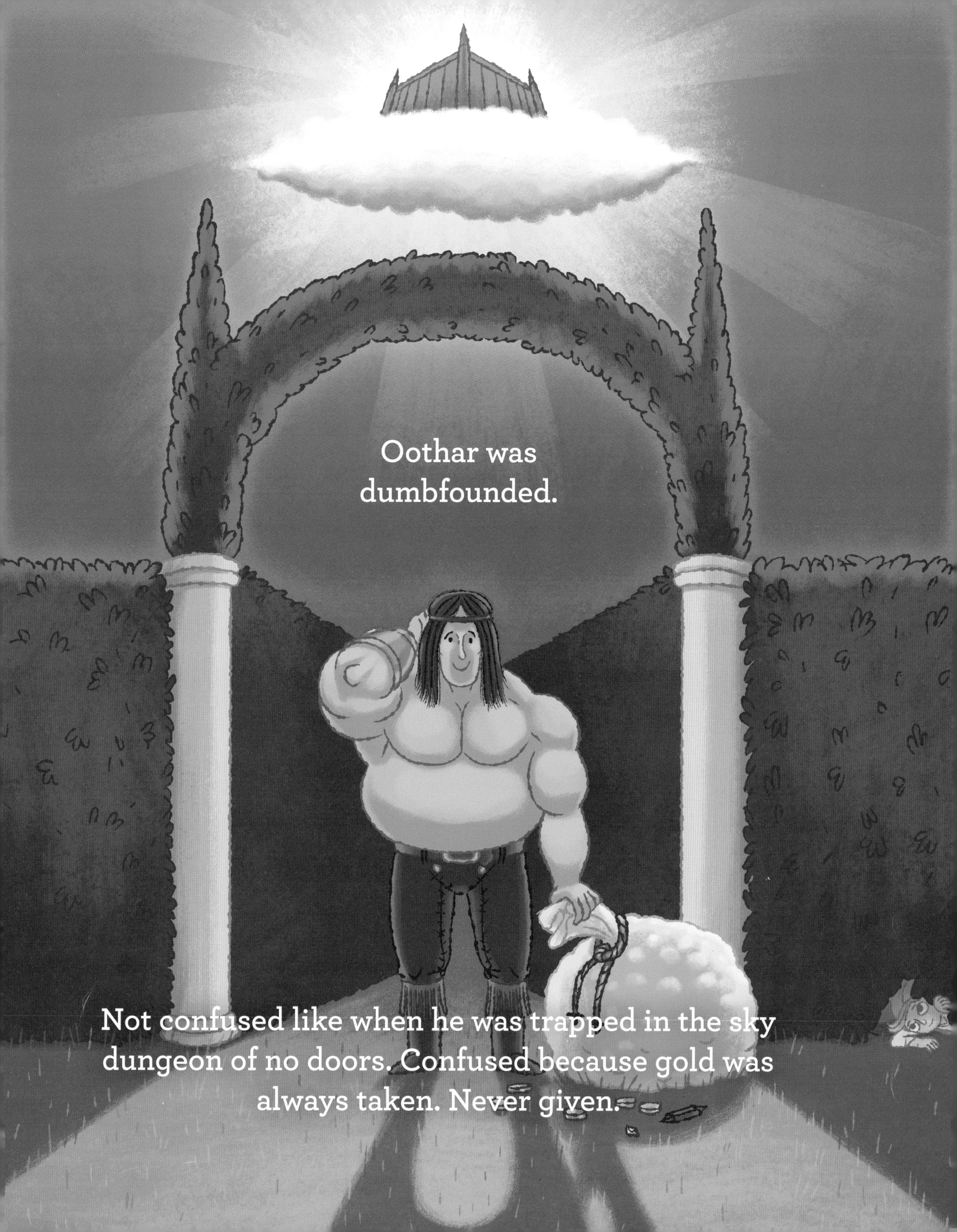

Oothar was
dumbfounded.

Not confused like when he was trapped in the sky dungeon of no doors. Confused because gold was always taken. Never given.

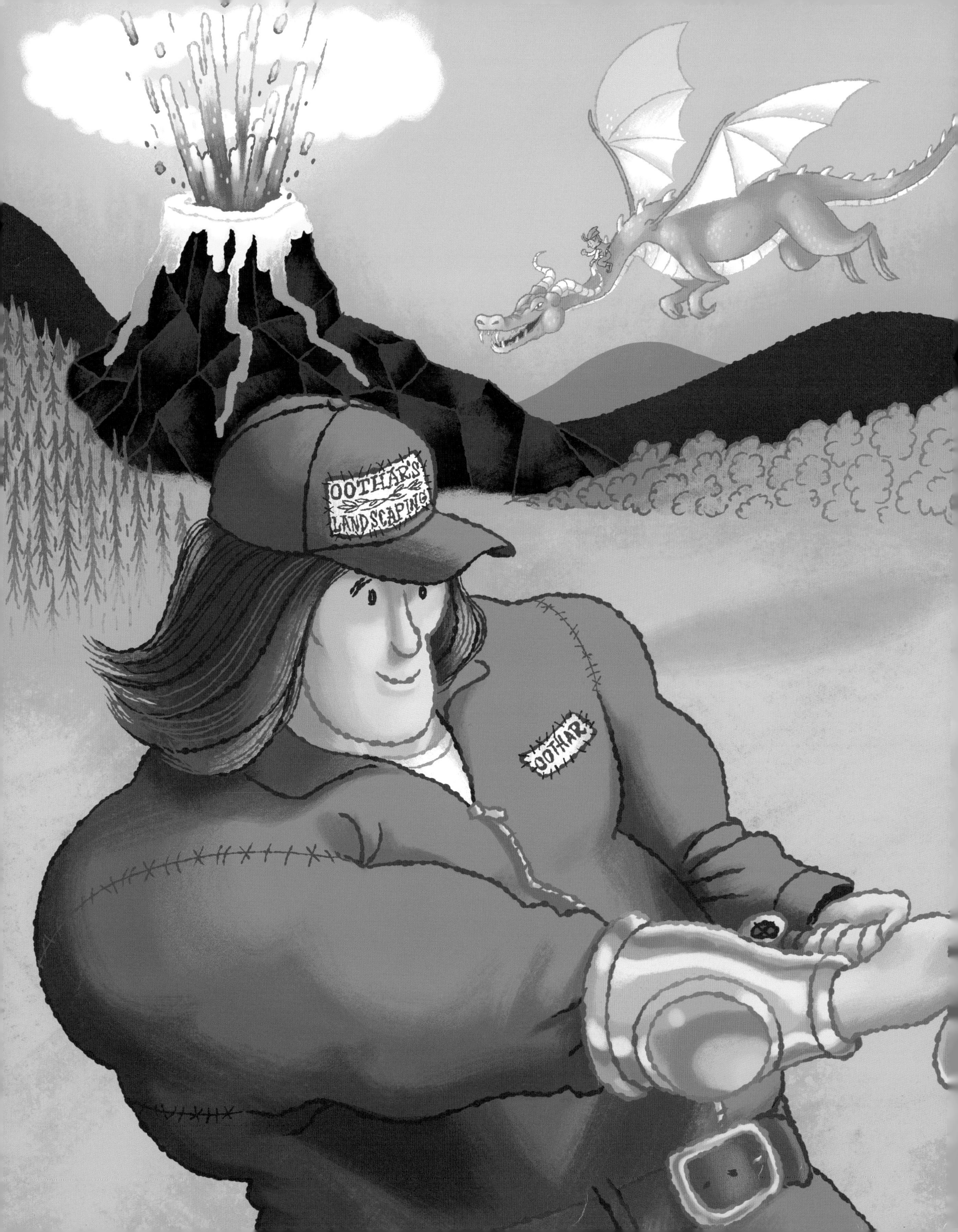
OOTHAR'S
LANDSCAPING
OOTHAR

Word of Oothar the Landscaper spread faster
than the molten ooze of Mount Sorrow.

And Oothar wasn't blue anymore.

No longer were his days spent battling ogres
and banishing uberwraiths. Instead, Oothar was
busy with hacking hedges and slashing weeds.

He was so busy...

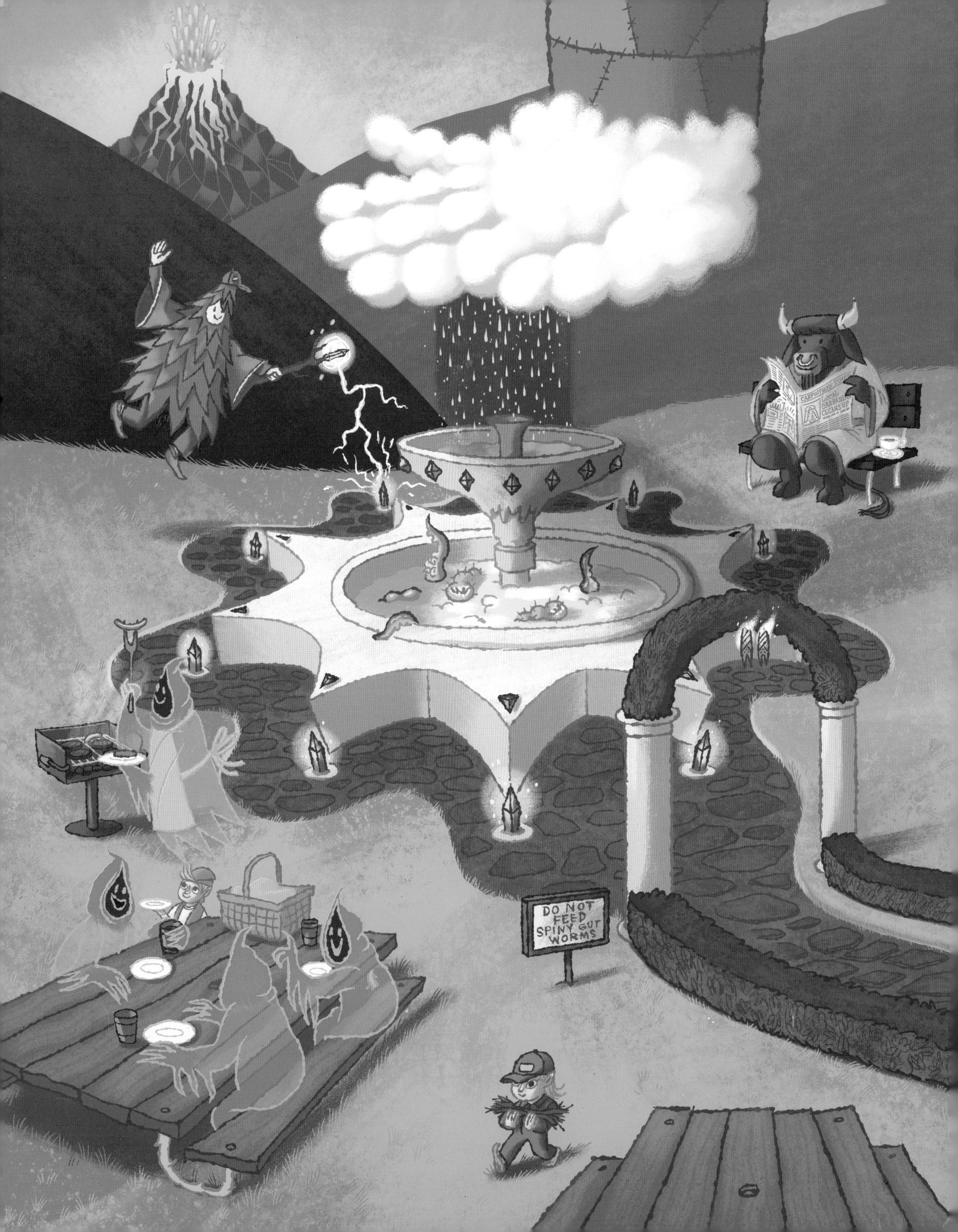
CARPOOTHIAN
LOCAL
CLEANS UP
DO NOT FEED SPINY GUT WORMS

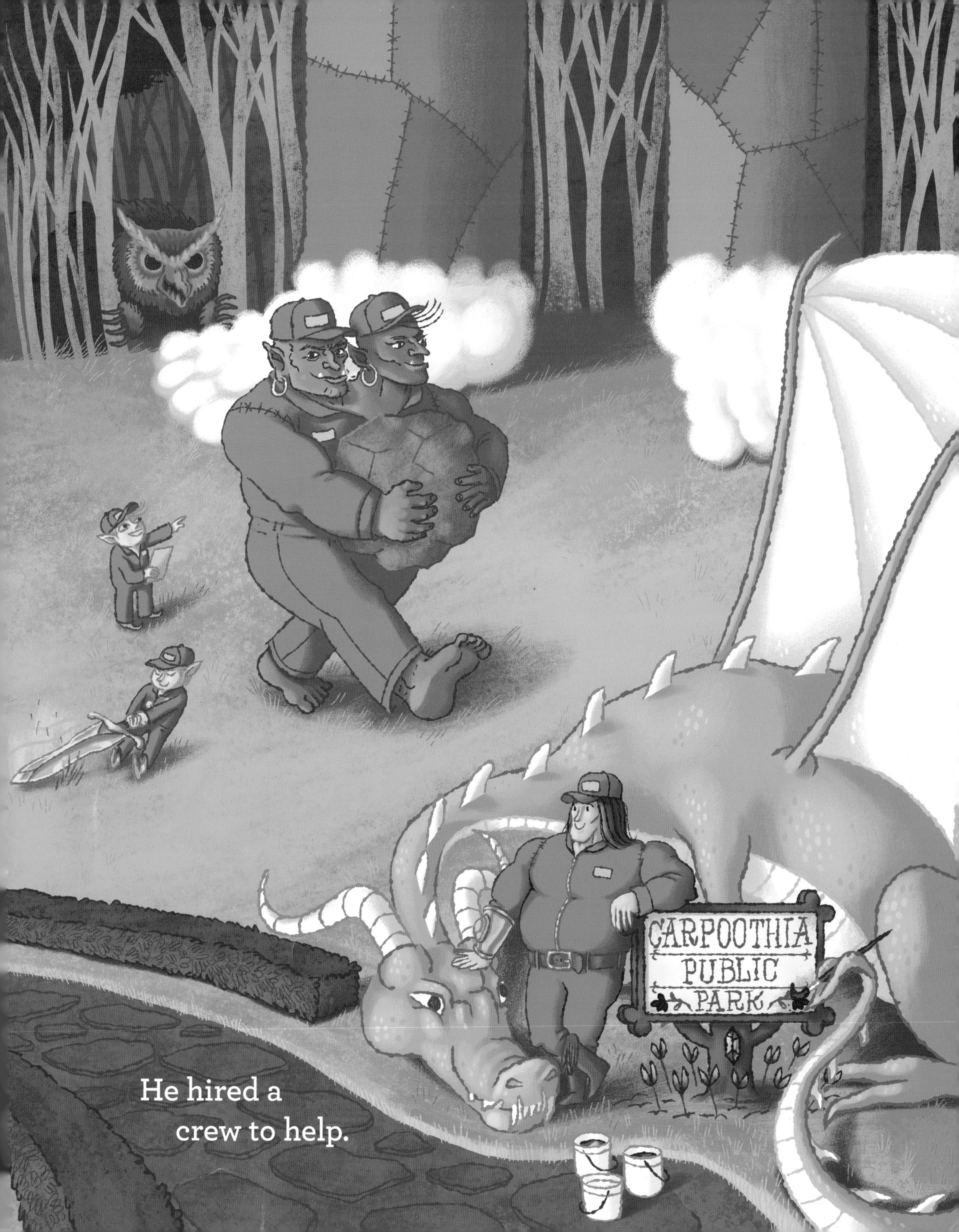
CARPOOTHIA
PUBLIC
PARK

He hired a
crew to help.

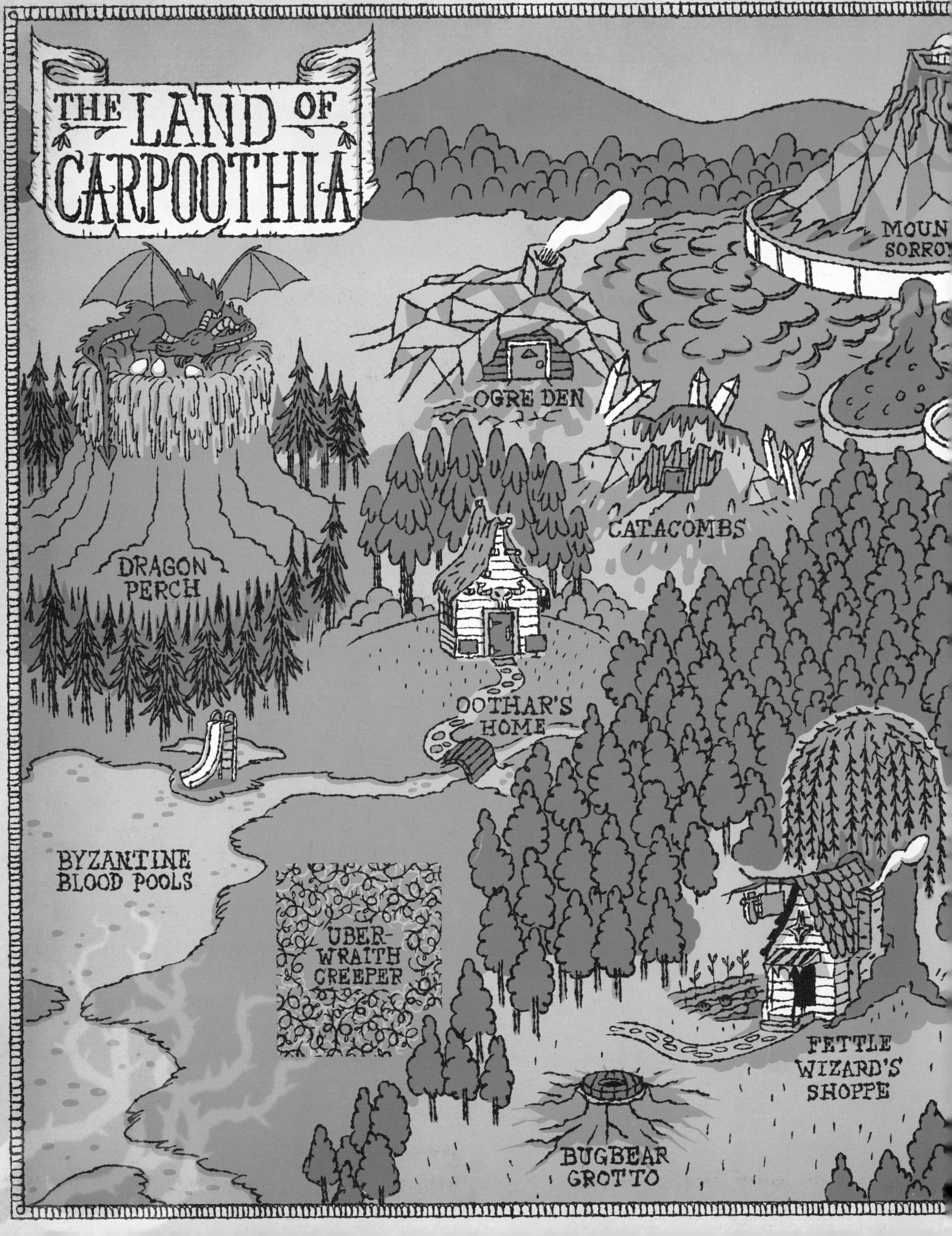
THE LAND OF CARPOOTHIA
MOUN
SORRO
OGRE DEN
CATACOMBS
DRAGON PERCH
OOTHAR'S HOME
BYZANTINE BLOOD POOLS
UBER-WRAITH CREEPER
FETTLE WIZARD'S SHOPPE
BUGBEAR GROTTO